Totally Bound Publishing books by BA Tortuga:

Roughstock Sweethearts
City Country
Picking Roses

Top of the Leader Board
Ace and Kitty

Roughstock Sweethearts

PICKING ROSES

BA TORTUGA

Picking Roses
ISBN # 978-1-78651-868-2
©Copyright BA Tortuga 2016
Cover Art by Posh Gosh ©Copyright January 2016
Interior text design by Claire Siemaszkiewicz
Totally Bound Publishing

Published in 2016 by Totally Bound Publishing, Newland House, The Point, Weaver Road, Lincoln, LN6 3QN, United Kingdom.

PICKING ROSES

Dedication

To my daddy, who would never let a lady stand on a
bus. You're my hero. BA

Chapter One

"I know it's tough, Rose, but we need you there."

Rose Cutrer nibbled on her cuticle, then stopped herself and shook her head, even though she knew the man on the phone couldn't see it, probably would ignore it if he could. No. No, she couldn't. She didn't want to go to Cheyenne. She didn't want to go back to the rodeo life.

She hadn't traveled much with Timmy when he'd ridden the circuit. She hadn't been the buckle bunny, short shorts and tank tops that showed everything type. Timmy had liked her for who she was. He'd loved her and he'd taken every opportunity he'd ever had to let her know. Hell, they'd dated for so long before they got married, and when it had finally happened…

Well, they'd only just started playing house when things had gone to hell in a handbasket. She'd gone from girlfriend to fiancée to wife to widow in the blink of an eye.

She pulled her finger out of her mouth again. God, years to break the habit and one single phone call brought it back in spades.

God, what a mess.

"I can't. I'm sorry, Ace. I just can't."

Presley jumped in her lap, her beautiful baby fuzzball yipping like he did whenever she got stressed out, then nuzzling her chin.

Ace Porter made a noncommittal noise. "Amy is really tore up, Rose. You could help her out a lot by supporting her. And there will be a real nice memorial for Timmy."

She sighed again, shook her head again. "Ace, I don't have the money. Traveling's expensive, and I'd have to board Presley. I'm only working part-time at the library—I don't get vacation time." Or sick time. Or anything.

"Well, now, don't get upset at me for suggesting it, Rose, but I'll pay for your trip. Flight and hotel and a spending allowance. I know it's a lot to ask, but I feel like I really need you there. You're so levelheaded, so calm."

Gracious, but Ace must be taking team-building lessons. Pep Talk 101.

"Y'all don't have something awful planned, do you? 'Cause I can't bear that." No fix ups. No blow-up, life-size Timmys. Nothing weird that would make her run or cry or puke.

"No, ma'am. I wouldn't do that to you." No. No, Ace Porter had been good to her. The head of the league, and Timmy had just been a low-level rider…

"I don't know. What would I say to her? I mean, I… It's just hard. That's it. It's just hard when they're gone."

Her bright-eyed, goofy Timmy had been there one minute and literally, the next, he was gone.

One bull, one hoof, one broken neck.

Poof. His light had been extinguished.

"Can I be blunt, Rose?" Ace waited for her murmured, "Mmmhmm" before going on. "You know how it is to be the one no one knows how to talk to. The wives can be a damned superstitious lot. They're afraid to talk to the one who's lost her man. She's so damned young, honey, and so scared."

"Yeah." Rose wasn't, not anymore. Christ, she was gonna be twenty-six in a few weeks. Twenty-seven.

Right. Twenty-seven.

God.

"Okay. Okay, Ace. If you'll foot the bill, I'll go. There's nothing I can say to her, though, that will make it better." Nothing. It hurt for a long time, every second, every breath, like hell. Then it got to be every few breaths. Nowadays it was this sneaky thing, like a sucker punch to the gut.

"I know that. It just means she won't feel so isolated." Ace heaved a sigh. "Did I ever tell you how sorry I am, Rose?"

"Yes, Ace. You did, and I appreciate it. Timmy... He would have done it anyway, even if he'd known. He loved riding bulls more than life."

More than her.

"The game gets in the blood, honey." Ace was grinning. She could just picture that lopsided dimple he had from a twice-broken jaw.

"That's what I hear. What are the dates you need me there again?"

"The first week of Frontier Days." They settled the rest of the business, Ace giving her the name and number of his assistant, who was going to call her about flights.

She said her goodbyes then hung up. Presley was right there, yipping and panting and worrying over her, just like he always did.

"I can't believe I have to do this, Pres. I mean, Timmy's gone. None of them want me around, not really, not without worrying…"

They all felt sorry for her. They all took care of her any way they could. But no one wanted the bull rider's widow around. No one.

Not even her.

Chapter Two

Rose stepped out of the La Quinta in Cheyenne, then walked over to Beau Lafitte, the famous bull rider standing there, just as wee and sturdy as ever. Retirement had done the man good, she could tell. "Mr. Beau! Ace didn't say you'd be here!"

Wyoming was sure pretty—all big sky and crisp wind, but she'd been feeling a little fish out of water since she'd arrived yesterday. That Amy gal hadn't made it through the first memorial deal—she'd collapsed before Rose got to meet her and was at the hotel with her momma, sedated. Rose, though, she'd stood through one and would stand through the second.

"Rosie! Hey, lady." Beau smiled, his one crooked tooth standing out a little. He stepped up and kissed her cheek. "How are you?"

"I'm okay. Good to see a familiar face, hmm?" she said. Beau had been Timmy's hero, and they'd spent a lot of time drinking beer with him and Sam Bell. Beau was the closest thing she had to family, being a Cajun and her from New Orleans. "You heading to the park?"

"I am. You?" He took her elbow, started walking her out to the parking lot.

"Yeah. I was waiting on the bus dealie." Her boots clacked on the asphalt. Tomorrow she was wearing flip-flops, damn it. All day. "How's Mr. Sam?"

"He's better all the time." Beau's traveling partner, Sam Bell, had been…broken up good. Right at the end of the last season. "Calling me to bitch every day about putting the dishes up too high."

"Poor guy. I hated that he got hurt so bad." She'd sent a card and couple of soft hats that she'd knitted, to help that poor busted head.

"He sure appreciated that you wrote." Beau took her to a big old pickup and opened the door. "I'll give you a ride, if you like."

"You don't mind?" The kids on that bus were rude and she couldn't comfortably reach the straps if she had to stand. Sucked to be short.

"Not one bit." He helped her on up just about the time AJ Gardner trotted up. "Miz Rose. Y'all mind if I ride in the bumper seat?"

"AJ." Lord, AJ was looking worn around the edges, and she'd bet dollars to donuts that he needed to spend a couple three weeks at home with his woman. "I don't mind if Mr. Beau'll have you."

"Come on, then." Beau grinned. "They didn't give you a rental?"

AJ shook his head. "Kynan and his crew took it last night to get burgers. Never brought it back."

"Lord, lord." They loaded in. "How's Missy and the kids?"

"Good. I mean, Missy is tired, but she's got a house-full. My oldest girl is starting to train to be a barrel racer, did you know?" He seemed so pleased. Missy must've been ready to whack him over the head.

"Is she? That's got to be exciting." Or terrifying. Pick one. Christ. She couldn't imagine having a little one racing at those speeds. She just wasn't that brave.

"Lord, yes. 'Fore long she'll be competing at her first event." AJ laughed, climbing in behind her.

Beau got them going, nodding along with the radio. It all seemed so normal.

She watched out the window. Timmy'd brought her here once. They'd spent all his day's winnings on the carnival, she thought. There'd been rides and games and greasy, awful food. He'd kissed her a lot that day and they'd gone out after the park had closed and drunk beer and danced like they were the only two people in the world...

She missed him, the lousy, rodeo-loving butthead.

Beau maneuvered them through the maze of trucks and SUVs, past the buses, back to the participants' parking. Oh, much better than the bus.

"Are you here for the memorial deal, Beau?" Lord knew she could use a friend up there in the middle of the arena.

"I'll be up there, yeah." He glanced over, eyes a slice of blue brightness among all the sun lines. "You holding up okay?"

"I guess. It's weird, seeing the footage of him. Last night they showed the wreck on the news, you know? I never want to see that again."

She'd been there when it had happened. He'd died in seconds. She hadn't even gotten to say goodbye, not really. He'd been gone before she made it to his side.

"I know it. Hell, we don't want to see stuff like that, and we wasn't married to him." Beau reached over and patted her hand, which was clenched on her thigh. "You've got my number in your little phone, right?"

"Yes, sir. I do." Beau was good people. Honest and dear.

"Well, if I ain't around or you cain't get to me, you call. Heck, text. I'll give you a ride back, all right?"

"Okay. Thank you, Mr. Beau, I appreciate it. I'm going to take it easy for the next two days. Wear flip-flops and explore." Be lazy.

At least until the big George Strait concert on Friday night.

"There you go! There's some cute shops downtown, Dillon says."

She'd never really gotten to know the clown, Dillon Walsh, but apparently he knew all the good places to go.

"That's what I hear." The shuttle stopped downtown, too, so she should be able to manage.

She glanced at her watch then sighed. "I have to go meet that girl from the newspaper. I'll see you at the memorial?"

"Yes, ma'am." He leaned over to kiss her cheek. "Call me if you need me."

"Thank you, sir." Rose squeezed his fingers, then took a deep, deep breath. One more thing then it was over and she could just tourist, maybe hang out with Beau or something.

Anything.

So long as she survived today.

* * * *

"Rose, this is Amy Martin. Amy, Rose Cutrer." Ace sounded solemn, looked it, too, standing with his hat in his hand.

The little gal was pregnant out to there and draped in black, tears rolling down her cheeks. "I'm sorry. I can't seem to stop. At least I made it here today."

"Hey, it's all right. Everyone's crying." She glared at the other wives a little, but none of them came up. God damn, it wasn't like dead was catching. You didn't doom your man to getting his head kicked in by hugging a widow. Rose took Amy in her arms and patted her back.

"You need to breathe, honey. Seriously. It's gonna be a long day." Rose gave Ace a nod then started heading Amy toward the little room they had set up—free drinks and tissues for the widows.

"Hey, y'all." Chrissy sat there already, all decked out in her sparkly blue shirt, prepared to ride. "Sorry that I didn't wear black, but Dougie hated it and I wear blue for him, every ride."

"No worries. Have you met Amy?"

"Mick's wife. No, ma'am." Chrissy stood, all damn near six feet of her. "I'm Chrissy Nail. My husband was killed in Iraq—he was a bullfighter when he wasn't called up in the Reserves."

"Oh." Amy sniffled. "I'm so sorry. Pleased to meet you."

"You too. There's Cokes and waters. It's damn dry here, y'all should drink up. God knows they're going to let this drag on forever."

Rose did love Chrissy—Chrissy'd been the one widow who had emailed her when Timmy had died, offering to come to her and take her to lunch.

The first thing Chrissy ever said to her was, "You didn't die, honey. Don't let anyone make you believe you should."

Now it was her turn to walk someone through the process, she guessed.

She grabbed two Sprites and Chrissy offered her a flask, just to get her through, but she shook her head. "In this heat? I'd hurl. I'm a lightweight."

"It'll rain in a bit. That will help." Chrissy chuckled. "Lord, you remember that time in Decatur in May?"

"Lake Wise County? I thought they were all gonna drown." She had to chuckle, had to. That bull riding had been sunk so hard in rain the bullfighters had been knee deep and wading. "Amy's man was a saddle bronc rider too."

Amy nodded. "He died at an event in Greeley. He wasn't even riding. He got kicked in the head."

"Everyone's got their time, I guess." Chrissy's mouth tightened and Rosie couldn't blame her one bit. No one wanted to be the one who lost someone, who had to tell themselves all the platitudes to get through the day.

"Yeah. Is this ever going to be over? I mean, will anyone ever want to be my friend again?"

God, Rose had asked herself that a thousand times, and the sad answer was, probably not here. She'd moved to Texas, found jobs, an apartment. There she'd met a ton of people who didn't know rodeo, didn't think she was Typhoid Mary.

She glanced at Chrissy, who rolled her eyes good-naturedly. "Sure, honey. You'll get to know new folks. I found a new church, and that helped. Rosie got herself a job."

"It will work out, sweetie. How far along are you?"

"Six months."

"That's a bitch," Chrissy said. "Everything seems huge."

"Especially my belly." Amy grinned suddenly, then they were all giggling together, just roaring with the stupid laughter borne from pain that cut all the way down to the bone.

Sometimes it felt good to cut loose.

Even if it did make a hundred cowboys stare at them.

Of course, when Chrissy stuck her tongue out at the lookie-loos, it just got worse. Or better. Or something.

Yeah. Yeah, okay. They could do this. They totally could.

Chapter Three

Les stretched his arms up, trying to work the kinks out of his upper back. That heavy little mare had nigh ripped his shoulders right out of his sockets. The shuttle bus was idling, the lights mostly off, every seat full. It was quiet, though. A man could have a nap.

The place was rocking back there, and more people were bound to come in before the old man at the wheel actually closed the doors and got them moving.

He caught a whiff of some serious BO, which led to pit sniffing, as clandestine as he could make it. Oh, not him. Good.

Sure enough, about the time the doors closed, a soft voice sounded and a tiny, fine-looking slip of a gal hopped on and paid her dollar. She headed for the back, moving careful, hunting for a place to light. When it was clear that there wasn't one, she reached up, fingertips barely catching the strap as she swayed on tiptoe.

Les stared at all of the young guns up front who weren't about to budge and let a lady sit down. Shit.

His momma had raised a cowboy, even if theirs hadn't. Unfolding his legs, Les stood and cleared his throat.

"Ma'am? Why don't you sit down?"

"Oh, that's—" The bus jerked and she tumbled forward, right against him. Les caught her and eased her down into his vacant seat. "Thank you, sir."

"Not a problem." He smiled down at her, just caught by her liquid dark eyes and the sad expression in them.

"They make buses for taller people." She winked, smiled at him.

"The handle parts at least, yeah." Wow. She was... Pretty didn't begin to cover it. "You're from down south, huh?" Her voice gave her away.

"Yes, sir. Longview, Texas, right near the Louisiana border."

"Ah." Well, then, she had to be disappointed in these rude-assed boys. Hopefully he'd made a better impression.

She pinked, glanced down, fingers playing with the bottom of the longest black-black braid he'd ever seen. "Are you from 'round here?"

"I'm from over in Colorado, but closer than you, I guess." Lord, she was something. He was glad it wasn't his body that was smelly. He wanted to make a good impression on her.

She nodded, blinked up at him again. Her throat was pale, slender, and he wanted to touch it. "Up in the mountains?"

"Yeah. Over by Steamboat Springs. Pretty up there." He paused, trying to remember how to make small talk with a woman. "Lots of moose."

"Moose? Like as in..." She put her hands up at her head, spread her fingers like antlers.

"Yeah. Like uh, Rocky and Bullwinkle... Only no squirrel." *Shut. Up.* Les. God, he was a dork.

She seemed surprised as she laughed, and the sound settled in the pit of his belly. "We have 'gators. No moose."

"I bet you got them weird swimming rats too." Hell, they had marmots in Colorado.

"Nutria? A couple three."

They stopped at the first hotel and the lady sitting beside the pretty lady moved and she scooted over. "Here. You sit."

"Thank you." She smelled nice. Her hair looked real soft. Les searched for a wedding ring. There was a wedding band — pretty and simple and gold, but it was on her right hand. Oh, man. He'd bet she was one of the gals in for the memorial, he'd bet. He'd seen a bunch of them, some riding the arena, some standing by the announcer.

Poor baby. He was enough of an ass to hope it had been a while, though. That she'd be ready to look at someone else. Maybe him.

"Do you know the town at all?" She had the biggest eyes.

"Come here every summer." Sometimes in between, too, depending on what there was going on.

"Do you know if there's somewhere to eat within walking distance of the La Quinta?"

"Walking?" Crap. The breakfast place next door wasn't an all-nighter. Those were all at least a mile or two away. Wait. This was good. "Nope. I know where you can get food this time of night, but it's not safe to walk. I could give you a ride."

"Oh, it's okay. I don't want to put you out. I bet I can make a meal from the vending machine." She jumped as her phone buzzed, and she answered it. "Hey, Mr. Beau. No, sir. AJ told me you were doing that reporter deal, so I caught the shuttle. You tell Sammy I said hi, huh? Yeah. Sleep well."

Beau. Shit. Beau Lafitte? Her husband must have been someone. Had to be Beau Lafitte if she was talking about AJ and Sam. They were all big time bull riders, way out of his tiny circuit league.

"Sorry. I was supposed to wait for a ride, but I didn't want to."

"Oh. Well, if you're meeting folks, then I won't bother you." Les screwed up his courage. "But if you'd like, I sure would be pleased to take you to get some food. I'm single, mostly sober, and I'm not one to abuse a woman's trust."

That laugh sounded again, low and musical. "I'm not meeting anyone. Beau was my husband's friend, and those men...they worry. Are...are you sure that you don't mind? Breakfast was a long time ago."

"I don't mind a bit." He hadn't had nothin' since before the rodeo, which had started at two. "I could eat a horse." Les chuckled. "Maybe the one that tried so hard to throw me."

Her smile faded, the tiniest bit. "Did you get hurt?"

"No, ma'am. She tried, but I had her number." He changed the subject. "I'm Les. Lester Jacoby." Les held out his hand.

"Please to meet you, Les." Her hand was cool, soft, smooth. "I'm Rose Cutrer."

Ah. Tim Cutrer's photo had been all over the arena, along with Mick Martin's and Dougie Nail, the bullfighter.

They hadn't ridden the same circuits most of the time, and Les rode broncs not bulls, but Les remembered Tim as a guy with a great sense of humor and a good sense of balance. "I'm sorry. About your husband, I mean. I only knew him a bit, but he seemed like a good man."

"Thank you. He loved his job."

"Yeah." Nice. Smooth. Make her think of the dead guy. Not classy. Les watched the lights go by for a moment, trying to think of what to say next.

She looked out the window too. "I keep trying to imagine it here in the wintertime."

"It's right pretty. Not as pretty as where I am." Steamboat was a winter wonderland, all slopes and valleys, covered in evergreen and white.

"That's neat. I grew up in New Orleans. It's not really snow country." She pronounced it 'N'awlins'.

"I went to New Orleans once." It had about killed him, the humidity and the smell of the river. Pretty, though.

"It's neat. Hot, though, and sticky." The La Quinta's lights came up and the shuttle swung into the parking lot. "There's my hotel... Are you here too?"

"I am. My truck's just right over there." Thank God. "Did you need to freshen up any?"

"No. No, I'm good." She glanced up at him. "Unless the mascara didn't make it through the day."

"You look real good." Without any real thought, he slid a hand around her waist, leading her to the truck. "Real fine."

"Good deal. You're sure I'm not putting you out, now, right?" Rosie hopped up in the truck, easy as you please.

"Not a bit. I'm peckish." Thank all hell he'd cleaned his truck. His sister Hester would call it boy-funk, all the stuff that built up in a man's truck.

Rose strapped herself in. "Pretty truck."

"Thanks. She's faithful." He grinned, patted the dash. "So, chain or local?"

"Whatever's the best. I'm starving."

"Okay." The place with the lady's name would have a much better late night menu than the chain, so he headed off toward the mall. Besides, it was bound to be quieter, too, not being right off downtown.

"So, do you do all the roughstock events or just the broncs?"

"I ride bulls sometimes. Not as good at it as I am the horses, but there's more money in it." Les glanced over. "Never made it to the big show, though."

"Timmy always said that was more who you knew than how you rode, in the bottom ranks."

"I reckon that's true." Les shrugged, turning off on the road that cut across town. "I only ride in the summer, really. Otherwise I'm at the ranch."

"Oh, you're a working cowboy — that's neat. We used to have a little place, but... Well, taxes and everything. I had to let it and the critters go." She pushed her braid back behind her, sat up straight. "I have a cute little apartment now, though, so it's all good."

That had to hurt. Les had never had his own place but most of his kind dreamed of it. "Well, I work for a big spread. Might have someplace of my own someday, though." The neon sign lit the way, and Les turned into the restaurant lot. There were plenty of pickups, but none that he recognized, so maybe they was safe.

He wanted her to himself.

"Oh, you're a big outfit man then? That's cool. All the old-school boys want to be you."

His cheeks heated a little, and he was just tickled as he could be. "Thanks. It's not glamorous, but I love it."

She slipped off her seat belt as he killed the engine. "That's what's important, isn't it?"

"It is. What all do you do?" She had to work, he guessed. Les hopped out and went to open the door for

Miss Rose. She had nice legs. Well, they looked sweet and lean in her skinny jeans, anyway.

"I work part-time for the water department doing the payroll and I work a couple hours a week at the library, doing story hour and stuff."

He knew that story, he reckoned. That was an 'I've been a Mrs., now I'm not' tale.

Bless her heart. She must be broke half the time. He didn't say it, though. "I always liked the bookmobile thing when I was a kid. I didn't get into town to the library much, though."

"Lots of folks don't, but I get to meet all the little ones, which is fun. I used to think I wanted to do that—be a librarian, but that's lots of schooling and I've done all of that I want to."

"I hear you." The place was fairly crowded, but Les got the little gal to give them a table toward the back.

In the light, Rose was even prettier, just as pale as milk, and she was rocking the redneck tuxedo, with her sparkly tank top and denim jacket. A tiny silver heart pendant nestled in the hollow of her throat. She had soft-looking lips, the lower one full and almost pouty, and her dark eyes were huge against her light skin. Lord, he was about to wax poetic. Too bad he couldn't rhyme anything but maybe horse and of course.

She ordered a glass of tea, then read the menu. "Man, I'm so hungry I could have one of everything."

"Well, you have whatever you want, Miss Rose." He was gonna have that cheese and egg thing, with toast, because they didn't serve biscuits this late.

"I think I'll have a waffle. They sound yummy."

Oh. Waffles. Damn, now he had to decide... He could have one on the side. With bacon. "Are you a syrup or honey gal?"

"I like syrup. You?" She had a beauty mark, tiny and dark, right under the corner of her lips.

"Syrup, definitely. Though I like strawberry jam sometimes."

"I love them with fresh strawberries and whipped cream, for dessert."

"Oh, that sounds good." Thank God she wasn't one of them girls who didn't eat, tiny as she was.

She smiled and her eyes twinkled. "It's decadent."

"Yum." Decadent, huh? That was more like...oh, chocolate frosting right out of the can. Fruit didn't qualify as bad for you, did it?

She nodded and curled her legs up underneath her.

Les stared, his coffee cup halfway to his mouth. She was so pretty anyway, but with her legs all back and stuff it pushed her perky little tits out.

"You okay?" She reached out, touched his knuckle. "Are you tired?"

"Huh? Oh. Oh, I'm fine." Les smiled and told the truth. "You're awful pretty, is all."

"Oh, now. I've been crying and stressed all day."

"Sure you have. Those memorial things is a bitch." He could remember when Kyle Frommer had died. The man had been a friend, and a damned good bull dogger, and Les had gotten all teary.

"They are. Ace called and asked me to come. He's hard to say no to."

"Ace." Oh, good Lord. She knew Ace Porter on a first name basis. He was the president of the whole bull riding association. "Guess he's hard to say no to. Can't say I'm unhappy that he got you here."

Oh, look at that pretty blush. God, he could just eat her up.

She opened her mouth, but the waitress came up to take their order, so he didn't get to hear it.

Rose got her waffle, and he got pancakes and eggs and bacon and potatoes. He was damned hungry. Les had to admit, he was a little hungry for her, but food would do.

He found out that Rose had been an only child, that her folks had died in Katrina, that she'd dated her husband for a long time before they got married. She didn't have any kids, she loved dogs, and she was named Rose after her granny.

They talked enough that he even told her about his life, which was a feat for him. He wasn't usually much of a talker. But he told her about his twin sister, who hated her name and went by Anne, which was her middle name. He called her Hes, maybe Hester Anne, just to rile her up. He told her about his mom and step-dad, who were somewhere in Mexico right now in their little aluminum trailer, seeing the ocean. He told her about his horses and his dog Iggy, who was huge and drooly and not at all like her petite baby named Presley.

They talked through food and tea, then coffee. Three cups worth.

Hell, they talked so much that he knew about her childhood bout of mumps and his bout of whooping cough. They'd had chicken pox at the same age, and he was two years older than she was. By like, three days.

"So, be honest, did you hate having your birthday during Christmas break during school?" Rose asked.

"Not too much. I mean, it sucked more that there was two of us and it was so close to Christmas that Mom and Dad couldn't afford two sets of presents." The bus had picked him and Hes up at like, six a.m. and dropped them off at almost seven at night. He hadn't missed school parties.

"Oh, man. I guess so." She poured a creamer in her warmed-up coffee. "I always wanted a sister or a brother. So, are you riding tomorrow?"

"Not tomorrow, no. I ride again on Friday." He cleared his throat, trying not to jiggle his leg like he did when nerves were about to get on him. "You, uh, you got plans?"

"Tomorrow? I'm going to wander downtown and explore a little. Ace got me tickets to the big concert Friday, standing room only, then I have Saturday to play and I'm home Sunday."

"Standing room?" Les frowned. "Friday is George Strait, ain't it? You won't see a thing."

"You don't think? Damn." She pouted a little, lips pooching out.

"Nope. It'll be crazy. I bet I could make a trade for some seats that have a good view." He made the offer sound casual, but man, he wanted her to go.

"Yeah? If I'm not going to see, I might as well be comfortable."

"Oh, you can see real well from some of the seats. Down there on the track, you'd get trampled." Les dared to reach out and touch her hand. "Let me see what I can do."

"You don't mind?" Shit, as tiny as she was... Hell, he'd be scared she'd get hurt—there were supposed to be ten thousand drunk people down there on the track.

"I don't mind one bit, honey. How many tickets did you need me to trade?" *Please say more than one.*

"I have two. I didn't have anyone to share with, but Ace wanted me to have an extra, in case."

"Oh. Well, I got me a nosebleed ticket because I wasn't sure I'd go. If I had someone to go with..." Was that rude? Inviting himself along?

"Do you think we could trade three tickets for two?"

"I bet I could." He'd finagle it somehow, if it killed him. "I'd be happy to pick you up. Unless you're coming on to the rodeo that day."

"No, I don't have tickets. I mean, I can wander the fair." She smiled at him like he was Christmas morning.

"I can come on about an hour before the concert and pick you up." He wanted to push to let him take her around the next day, too, but he didn't want to spook her.

"Oh, that would be neat. I'll buy supper, after, if you want."

"That would be fine. Real fine." Lord, he was tickled pink as Pepto.

"Cool." She scribbled a number down on a piece a napkin. "This is my number. If you need the tickets or something."

"Thanks, honey." Les figured he'd best return the favor. He pulled out a little card from his wallet and handed it over. He'd had them made up when he was doing handyman work in Steamboat a year or so ago. "There's my cell. Call me if you get bored tomorrow and want to go see a movie or some such."

She took the card, put it in a glittery pink wallet. "Thank you, Les. You've been so dear."

"It's been my pleasure." It really had. He couldn't remember ever liking a woman's company more in such a short time.

He could only hope he'd get a chance to see more of her in the next couple of days.

Chapter Four

Rose headed downstairs closer to noon than eleven, hoping to catch the bus to town. She'd been up later than she'd been in five years, and when she'd fallen asleep, she'd dreamed about Timmy, her pocket cowboy with his dark, laughing eyes.

Of course, when she got downstairs, it was a very different Wrangler butt she saw standing by the bench outside. Les, her dinner cowboy from last night.

He was tall and blond, with shockingly blue eyes that rested on her like she was so fine. Too bad he was a cowboy just like her Timmy. Summers only or not, he rode the rodeo.

She smiled at him, waved when his gaze caught her. "Morning."

"Hey, there. You heading into the park?" Les' eyes lit with a bright pleasure when he looked at her.

"I was going to go hunt for food and then maybe wander downtown. You?"

"That was my plan too. I could chauffeur." He held out a hand, natural as anything.

"You don't mind?" She slipped her hand in his, her smile going wide.

"Not one bit." He tugged her out into the sunshine, heading for his truck.

"Thank you. Did you get some rest?"

"I did. I slept good." His cheeks pinked, but he didn't give any indication that it was a bad thing.

"Good deal." She was much more comfortable today—jeans and layered tank tops, flip-flops and her hair in a long ponytail.

"So what are you hungry for? I bet you get Mexican at home. They got this great pizza place." His truck was a shiny gray in the daylight, with a cling sticker on the pass-through window that said, "Let 'er Buck."

"I love pizza." Rose settled in and grinned at Les. She wasn't doing anything wrong, spending time with this guy. Hell, there was no telling—Beau or AJ might've asked him to look out for her. That would be sad, but life could disappoint and she might as well enjoy it now. "If that works for you, it works for me."

"I do too." His eyes slid over to meet hers right before he pulled out. "You don't like anything weird on it, do you?"

"Pepperoni. Mushrooms if they're not slimy. You?"

"I like meat. Onions if I'm not gonna offend. Maybe mushrooms." Those tanned hands handled the truck like nothing going. "Looks like we're good."

"Boys always like meat on pizza." She'd never met a cowboy one that didn't. Meat and jalapenos.

"Well, sure we do." His hat tilted to one side, a sure sign of a cowboy trying to think. "Unless they're a sissy vegetarian man."

Rose wasn't sure she'd ever met a guy who was a vegetarian. "I think you have to be famous and into yoga for that."

"Yeah?" They pulled into a little shopping center. "There was this guy I knew once who was a cameraman for the finals rodeo. He only ate tofu."

"Ew." Her nose wrinkled. Dillon Walsh ate tofu once at a Chinese restaurant. Timmy said Gramps Pharris and Nate had filled the clown's shorts with the weird stuff for the whole rest of the event.

"Yeah." Grinning, he pulled in at the front of a little place that already smelled like tomato and garlic by noon-thirty. The joint was busy, too, with families and cowboys and teenagers going in and out. It didn't take too long to get a table, though, and the music was solid, classic country.

"Thanks, ma'am." Les had manners, at least. He was so nice to the hostess that they got bread and water right away instead of waiting for the waitress. Not flirty nice, just nice.

She sipped her water, watching all the different kinds of cowboys wandering around — from goat ropers to Texans, mountain cowboys and redneck wannabes. Big rodeos brought them out of the woodwork.

Good thing she wasn't into rodeoing.

Or cowboys.

"So, you want to share a pizza, hon? Or do you want a lunch special?" Les had taken off his hat and put it brim up in the chair next to him. His hair was cut ruthlessly short, and it was either prematurely gray or so sun-bleached that it was all white.

"We can share." Was that too familiar? She chuckled at herself. *Jesus, Rosie. Get a grip. You're making a friend. Relax.*

"Oh, good." He gave her a raised brow expression. "Now the most important question. What kind of crust do you like?"

She chuckled. "If it's crunchy on the bottom, thick. If it's going to be gooey, then I'd rather have thin. You?"

"I like the thick, but I'm like you. No goo. They do buttery goodness here." Les nodded at the waitress, who came to take their order right away.

They ended up with pepperoni thick crust, two Cokes, and an order of fried cheese to split. "God, it smells like heaven in here," Rosie said.

"Heaven is a steakhouse in Omaha, honey. I've been there. This is good, though." He laughed, stretching his arms up over his head.

She liked the way his shirt stretched over his belly, liked the way his arms bulged. His hands were tan like his face, but she could see his arms were pale up under the shirtsleeves. Working man's tan. Timmy didn't have that—he had been a sun worshipper and a wild child. She was surprised to find Les' farmer's tan just a little bit hot.

"Do you like steak?"

"I do, but only if someone else cooks it. It makes me a little queasy, touching it raw." She blushed, rolled her eyes at herself. "I know it's silly, but true."

"Well, as long as you like it, it's all good." *Look at that smile.* He was really something else. Not that she went for his type.

Nope.

No cowboys.

"So, what about you? Do you like sweets?" She loved to bake—she told herself, when she got a chance, she'd go to pastry school in Shreveport, maybe. Even if she hated school.

"I like the ones with fruit, you know? Apple strudel. Cherry pie."

"Mmm. Cherries." She nodded, smiled at the waitress when the fried cheese came. "Oh, man. If Presley was here, he'd be having a fit to get to the cheese."

"Your dog, right?" Those long fingers snagged a piece of the cheese, but Les dropped it right back on the platter. "Whoa, hot."

"Don't burn yourself, now..." She handed him a napkin. "Are you okay?"

"I have a blister." Holding up his index finger, Les chuckled. "You could kiss it better," he teased.

"Goodnight..." She took his hand, tutting around the blister, touching the area gently. "Man."

"Gotta watch that melty cheese, huh?" His voice sounded a little scratchy all of a sudden.

"You *do*, Les. What if you'd just bitten into it? Ow. Your poor mouth would be all burnt."

"Yeah." His fingers curled around hers and squeezed a moment before he sat back and let go. "Red sauce smells good, huh?"

"It does." She sat back, snagged a cheese stick with her fork, cut it up to let the steam out.

Those blue eyes never left her, Les watching her as if she was about to do something amazing. It could have made her twitchy, but it didn't seem strange, somehow. Rose smiled at him, dipped her bite, and hummed over the flavor. Oh, man. So crispy outside and creamy in, with a sting of acid-y tomato.

"Yum." He blinked, then chuckled and served him up a bite, finally glancing away. His cheeks were all pink under his tan again.

"So, when did you ride your first horse?" She knew cowboys and, even if they didn't like riding, like her Timmy, they had a story about it.

"I don't remember, really. First time I rode alone I think I was maybe five. I mean like without someone holding the reins." This one liked to ride. She could tell by the way his eyes lit up when he talked about it.

"Yeah? I was a little older—maybe eight. I had a little buckskin at my grampa's." Buck had been mean as a snake and toothy as fuck, but they'd had an agreement.

"I have a pretty little mare up at the ranch. I ride all of the ranch remuda, but she's mine. Quarter horse mustang mix." Les seemed so proud. He was adorable.

"Oh, how neat! What's her name?"

"Scamp. She can be something else." Les split the last cheese thingee to share with her.

"Thank you." She licked the grease off her fingers. "Do you know how to ski? Do they let you live in Colorado if you can't ski?"

"I do. Know how, I mean. I'm not sure about the Colorado ski law, but in Steamboat they teach it in school." Their pizza came, and Les moaned a little. "Oh, smell that."

Rose chuckled. Boys did love their pizza. "Are you sure Heaven's in...was it Idaho?"

"Nebraska. Of course, there's a pizza place in Idaho Springs, Colorado that might be close. They have a salad bar to die for." Bless him, he pulled a piece out for her first, then himself.

"Thank you." She sprinkled red pepper on hers. "There's a barbecue joint near me that has a salad bar. It has amazing chocolate pudding."

"Does it? Do they have good brisket? I remember that about the summers I spent on the Texas circuit." He didn't salt or pepper, he just dug in, dipping the tip in the leftover sauce from the fried cheese.

"They do. Sausage too. So you ride in the summer and are a working cowboy in the winter?"

"Mostly, yeah. Sometimes I get work up in Montana in the summer, but I make more money riding the circuit. I get the horses pretty well. The bulls I'm not such good friends with." Les licked his fingers, too, totally at ease.

"I've never been to Montana. Tim…my husband, he loved to ride there. Won the event there twice."

"It's big sky." Long fingers reached out and snagged a pepperoni off her pizza. It had been dangling off the side anyway.

"Thief!" She chuckled, stuck her tongue out at him. "Snatching a girl's pepperoni!" Man, that sounded dirty.

"It was a dangler." Les blinked at her a moment, then hooted. They both laughed hard enough that the whole restaurant stared, but it was okay. She hadn't had a hard laugh in too long.

They finished off the pizza in record time, both of them patting full bellies. "We ought to go downtown and walk it off, huh?"

"Sounds like a plan." She stole the bill from under his hand. "You got supper last night."

"Oh, now, you don't have to, honey. You're taking me to a concert tomorrow." He stole it right back.

"Les… You have to promise to let me buy your beer tomorrow, then."

"I can do that." Les paid the bill and left the waitress a nice tip before they headed out and drove downtown, before parking in the nice big parking garage they had down there. Les chatted at her the whole way… Well, he had her chatting, asking her questions to keep her going.

They headed down into the sunny afternoon, her hand on the crook of his arm. All the stores were open and the depot was filled with little vendors.

"Where to first, honey? Looks like the western wear place is having a sale."

"I don't want to bore you to death, but..." She chuckled, pointing at the mechanical horse sign that was galloping at the top of the store. "Oh, *look!*"

"That's a local icon, huh? Been there for years. 'Sides, I could use a female opinion on a new pair of Wranglers."

"Opinions I'm good at." And admiring cowboy butts. She'd admired thousands. "I need to hunt for a shirt to wear to the concert, too." Something nice and crisp and pretty.

"There you go. You got any good dancin' boots?" His hand slid down to grab hers, and he twirled her into a little turn, right there on the sidewalk, making her feel like Cinderella.

Oh, wow. And also, yay. "I do. I love to dance."

"Good deal. They got an after party tent where the dancing is pretty tight. We could go after the concert." Les dipped her in a shallow swing.

She peered at his face, just to make sure he wasn't just being nice. He sure seemed pleased.

"That sounds like a ball, Les." She leaned up, kissed his cheek. "Thank you."

A big smile dawned on his face, and he nodded, tucking her arm back in to take her across the street. "You're welcome, Miss Rose."

The store was a madhouse—cowboys and girls and sales people running amok, a line for the bull riders' signing going down the center. She nodded at AJ and Packer, then grinned as bullfighter Coop jumped up to hug her.

"Rosarita! Sweet girl. Nattie said Beau mentioned you were in town."

She hugged Coop tight. He'd broken a hip trying to save Timmy, and had appointed himself her protection when Beau and Sammy weren't around. "I am. I'm shopping."

"Good on you. You need anything? Ace is taking care of you?"

She nodded. "Ace is. Beau is. Les is. Y'all are making this a wonderful trip."

"Les?" Coop peered over her shoulder. Les was right there, even if he was hanging back a tiny bit, shifting from foot to foot.

"He's a bronc rider. He's showing me around." She smiled back, held out one hand for the dear man.

"Hey, Mr. Cooper. Les Jacoby." Les came right up and shook Coop's hand, his other hand landing on her waist.

"I've seen you ride. For someone with long old legs you do all right. Pleased. You be careful with our Rosarita, now. She's tiny."

"I am not," Rosie said, then poked out her chin.

Coop winked at her. "Shit, baby girl, you're littler'n Jason Scott."

"I'll treat her right." Les chuckled, gave her a squeeze. "She's good at standing up for herself, I'd bet. She knows her own mind."

"That she does. I got fans. Y'all be good." Coop slipped her a receipt. "Here. This is good for a hundred dollars' worth of clothes. Have fun."

"Coop!" She couldn't take that.

"Gotta go." Coop waved and went back to the table.

Les just swung her around and headed her toward the girly shirts. "Looks like you got some big brothers, huh?"

"I do. After my folks died, then Timmy, they just worry. It's nice to have family."

"It is. Good on you, honey." Les leaned close to her ear, laughing a little, but not mean at all. "Rosarita."

She rolled her eyes. "At least it wasn't Rosie Posie, hmm?"

"I like Rosie." He paused a moment. "'Less your husband called you that. Then it might be awkward, huh?"

Rose smiled. "Timmy called me Robbie. My middle name is Roberta and his was Robert."

"Well, that's cute as hell." Les squeezed her again before letting her go. "Now, you need to find a sparkly shirt that will go from concert to honky tonk."

"And you promised to give me a Wrangler butt fashion show." Oh. Oh, man. She was flirting, like officially flirting. Rose felt downright giddy.

"I did. So I guess we got to take turns." Les glanced around and found an unoccupied seat over by the dressing room, which was a minor miracle. "You first."

Chapter Five

Les sat next to Rosie at the theater, digging popcorn out of the bucket she held on her lap. He'd tried to be a gentleman and hold it, but when she got all wrapped up in the movie and started digging around…

Well, his tight new Wranglers got a lot tighter, and he was sure afraid he'd embarrass himself.

They'd agreed on an action movie — one silly enough that it had her laughing, gory enough that she hid her face in his shoulder at the bloody parts. She was soft and warm and her dark hair smelled like flowers. Otherwise, she kinda smelled like steak and onion blossoms, but he was a cowboy. That worked for him too.

They'd played all day — shopped and walked, had a beer, shot a game of pool, then walked some more. Hell, he'd walked more today than he had in ages. The girl had legs on her for someone so small. Legs and a fine ass and the prettiest little figure. And her mouth…

Men had gone to war for less than those soft, red lips.

He shifted, a little uncomfortable again. Damn, he needed to get past that, his need riding him like a bronc rider with no paycheck.

"You okay?" Her breath tickled beneath his ear as she whispered.

"Mmmhmm. My jeans are kinda snug. You saw to that, huh?" They'd gone back to the hotel to freshen up a bit before supper and a movie, and he'd wanted to impress her.

"They suit you, sir, down to the ground."

"Thanks, honey. I like the shirts you picked out, too." They made her boobs look amazing.

She smiled against his cheek, then settled against him, eyes back on the movie. Lord. He was in way too deep to be seeing a lady who was leaving town in a few days. *Right? Right. Christ.*

Still, when her hand slid into his, their fingers twining together, he thought it was too late to stop falling.

Les just kind of held her hand and leaped into the void. He'd never been one to question his fate, really.

The good Lord brought her to him—he'd just have to make sure he got to keep her somehow. Good thing Les wasn't a bit afraid of hard work, and he had his share of grit. Yes, sir.

Chapter Six

His rigging felt as solid as it ever had. His neck brace was on snug, and Les knew his preparation was at least as hardcore as his perspiration. He'd drawn a third generation rodeo mare, a bay with a spotted rump who'd won Bard Natrum ten thousand in Austin back in March.

Time to pull his hat down like old Chris LeDoux and ride this sucker.

"Ride this bitch, Les, man. You can do this." Grundy grinned at him, the broken teeth making him look like a jack-o-lantern.

"You know it." Les grinned wildly in return. He tugged up on his rigging, making sure nothing gave, then bent his knees and raised his boots. That was when he nodded his head, ready for that gate to swing.

The gate popped wide and he lifted his legs to mark out, heels up over the horse's shoulders. He had to stay in that position for the first leap or he'd get a no score.

Disqualifying wasn't going to happen today. He needed a purse, dammit. A check so that he could wash his truck and take Rosie for a steak. Les gritted his teeth, his head snapping back with the force of the mare's initial leap.

Damn. He held on, eyes rolling back in his head as he focused on keeping his ass in the middle and finding this bitch's rhythm. He had to spur, so he got his legs moving, up and down, his back hitting her hard ass with every buck. His spine rattled like an old Halloween song about them bones.

The eight seconds on the back of Sunspot was like a hundred years in real time, that old girl's arched back and stiff kicks making him work up a sweat.

The whistle finally blew about the time Les thought his teeth would rattle out even with the mouthguard in place. He pulled himself upright, then turned his head, searching for the pickup man.

One of the Taggart triplets was right there, and Les grabbed hold of the lean waist, letting the man and momentum drag him off the horse. He ended up with his boots on the dirt, running a few steps alongside the horses before he broke away and caught up with himself enough to stop.

The crowd was cheering like mad fools and the eighty-two points on the ride was going to keep him in the money. He pumped his arms for the rodeo fans before trotting over to grab his rigging off the arena floor.

He wiped his forehead off, then went to get his bag before he checked his phone.

There were two texts—one from his sister that said, *Good ride,* and one from Rosie that said, *Take care of yourself.*

He didn't blame her one little bit for not wanting to be there, to go through watching someone ride, but it felt damn good, knowing she was thinking of him. Fine as frog hair and twice as hard to find, the feeling Rosie gave him.

He texted back. *Where you at?*

The fabric shop picking up my best friend a gift. U done?

I am.

His body was letting him know he wasn't all that young, damn it, his joints and muscles beginning to ache. Maybe he ought to check in with sports medicine and get an aspirin.

The text bubble came up, disappeared, then returned. *Wanna get together??*

Heck yes.

He wanted to see all of her that he could. Or as often as he could. Whatever.

His phone rang seconds later, Rosie's number popping up. "So, where would you like to meet? I can catch the bus in half an hour."

"I can meet you out front at the gates."

"Good deal. I'll be there with my shopping bag. I've been playing."

"See you soon, honey. Can't wait." He could put her bag in his truck. Trying to drive out of the park and find a place to park when he got back would be a nightmare.

This worked just as well as going to take her out. This way he could drive her back to the hotel after they ate and goofed off, wandered a little bit. There was a lot to see.

He waited for her, nodding to people as they passed, but really wanting to see nothing but a pretty dark-haired lady in... Oh, a red sundress that looked like heaven. Les stared because he could, at least until she saw him. Lord, she was fine. She had on big, dark sunglasses and a silly little crushable hat, sparkly flip-flops and Lord help him, he was stupid over her.

Les moved, his feet taking him right to her. "You're looking good this afternoon, Rosie." He felt like a hound dog on a trail, unable to stop moving.

"Hey, cowboy! I went shopping and found little Western fabrics for Lindsay's baby. Her mom's making a quilt for the baby shower."

"We can lock it in my truck if you want." He took her arm and bent to kiss her cheek.

"That would be great, thank you. How was your ride?"

"Good. Ended up in the money for the go round, which helped out a lot." She smelled so good, like flowers and woman. Les breathed deep, worried now that he smelled like horses and sweat.

"Oh, congrats! That means you can have the extra-long corny dog for supper." Her smile lit up her whole face, her dark eyes sparkling.

"And spiral fries." Les winked. "I do love fried stuff."

"I am figuring that out." She took his arm, her touch just right. "Shall we wander? Look at the neat things?"

"I think so." They managed to get her cloth put away in the truck, then headed back in the main gates, stopping at the Dodge vehicles and the big hat outfit to get Les' hat steamed and brushed.

"Holler when you're hungry, cowboy. There's a lot of you to feed." Rosie winked when she said it, flirting playfully in a Southern way that made Les worry he would spring a happy.

"Oh, now, I'm always ready to eat, but I can nibble along until you're ready." Hell, he was tickled he knew what the question was.

"Good deal." She leaned a little and he felt the press of her breast against his arm, soft and giving and he wanted more.

He could get used to this. He surely could. Les hummed along with the song blaring over the speakers and guided Rosie toward the big retail building.

God, shopping on purpose and enjoying it.

He had it bad.

Grinning, he tugged her through the doors into the air conditioning, thinking how soft her hair seemed, how good she smelled.

They goofed off like teenagers, checking out stamped leather belts and the sharpest knives in the world, new pigging ropes and Egyptian cotton sheets.

"Look at that couch," Rosie said, pointing out a leather sofa with cowhide down the sides. "That costs more than my rent for a quarter."

"Iggy would just chew on it." His big slobbery baby loved anything with rawhide on it.

"Gracious, that would a shame." Rosie petted the couch. "Pres would just nap a lot and get white hair all over it."

"Mmm. Better put a blanket on it then." He steered her on and they stared at a bunch of huge photographs of canyons in Utah before turning the corner.

"Candy!" Les wiggled his fingers like a little kid. One stand had hundreds of types of classic dime store candy for sale.

"Oh, do they have those peppermint sticks?" Rose grinned and grabbed one and a caramel apple candy log too.

"They have root beer candy and red hots." They were selling by the pound, so Les got them a bag and filled it with their goodies, weighing it down.

Les laughed as Rose squealed over the sweets—rock candy and cherry sours and lemon drops. By the time they had a huge bag filled and checked out, they decided it was time for corny dogs and curly fries. "We must be hungry if we got that much candy, huh?"

"We must be." She chose a cinnamon candy out of the bag and raised it to his lips.

Les nipped it out of her fingers, his heart racing when she touched his mouth. Just that much of a touch excited more than full-on naked with some ladies.

"Oh." She blinked up at him, her dark eyes the warmest things he'd ever seen.

God, he wanted to kiss her, wanted to see if her mouth yielded to his, if she would be surprised or hungry for him too. He found himself dipping his head, wanting to taste the sugar on her lips, the cherry ChapStick.

Rosie lifted her chin as if she was going to kiss him right back, and he put one hand on her hip, steadying them both, when someone knocked into them, bumping him good and almost causing him to lose their candy.

When he glanced back down at Rose, she was blushing and hiding from him some, staring at light-up flowers made out of beer cans. Les took a deep breath and munched his candy. They needed supper.

They needed to not do this here in the middle of the whole world.

Maybe later, after the carnival and the stock show and dark falling and some cotton candy... Rosie was worth every moment. No rushing. No accidents.

When the moment came for him to taste her finally, Les wanted to take his time. He wanted to give Rosie the best first kiss ever. He wanted her to know he meant it.

Chapter Seven

Come on, sleepyhead! Look at you, sleeping in!

The chime on her phone made her laugh out loud. Beau had started texting at nine, wanting to get together, but she'd ended up at the Village Inn until after three a.m., drinking coffee and talking Les' ear off.

She'd finally managed to be up and ready by fifteen 'til to have an eleven o'clock lunch, she hoped.

Shut up, old man, she sent back.

Oh, now, I'm getting younger every day.

Where are you? she texted.

Down in the lobby.

I'll be right down.

Rosie slid on her flip-flops and scooted out to the elevator, feeling lazy as anything.

Beau stood in the lobby, solid as a rock, signing an autograph for a young fan.

Rose hung back until the wee one moved off, but then she hugged her fellow Cajun tight. "How's Sam today? Better?" she asked.

"He is. Grumpy that he's missing all the action. How are you?" He kissed her cheek gently and led her out to his truck. He loaded her up in the passenger seat, such a cowboy that.

"Good. I was up late, chatting with someone." Her cheeks heated.

"Like on the 'puter?" He sounded surprised, and she couldn't blame him. She wasn't online much.

"Nah. Like at the Village Inn." Laughing and blushing and touching hands over the tabletop.

"No shit? Pardon my French."

"Yeah. I met a guy. Les Jacoby."

"Saddle bronc rider?" Beau said, eyes narrowing.

"Bareback." She shivered, arms wrapped around herself. She hated the thought of those sharp hooves. "Although he's mostly a working cowboy, a big ranch."

"Ah, just rodeoin' for the hell of it?" Beau nodded sagely. He respected working cowboys, which some rodeo men didn't.

"Yes. You boys and your games." She had to tease, had to. Mr. Beau had retired from bull riding, wasn't on the circuit at all, and from all he said, didn't miss it. That was unusual in its own right, as most cowboys couldn't give up the ride until injury forced then to. Though she guessed Mr. Sam's injury had done that for Beau right enough. The two men were...together.

"Yep. I'm doing fantasy baseball right now. Got to keep busy." His warm chuckles made her laugh too. "I was thinking Old Chicago's."

"Sounds perfect." Timmy had loved the beer flights at the Italian brewpub. "Fantasy baseball? Seriously? That's cool. How are you doing?"

"I'm shit at it. Sam made some good picks." He turned off the main road from the parking lot. "I'll do better with football."

"You are a Cajun." They pulled out onto the highway and headed into town. "It's been a neat vacation. I'm going to see George Strait tonight."

"Oh, King George. Nice."

"Yeah. You going?" she asked. He would probably get to meet Mr. George if he went.

"Nah. Sammy's missing me and I'm driving back after we lunch." Look at that smile. Someone wanted to go home.

"Oh. Oh, did I slow you down?"

"No, ma'am. I wanted to sit and jaw with you while I have the chance." He never made her feel as though she was a bother. Not once.

She reached out, squeezed his wrist. "You're good to me, Mister Beau."

His cheeks pinked right up. "Aw, now, I just like your company."

"Good, because I'd cry if you gave up on me now. Tell me everything about home." Sometimes she missed Louisiana so bad, but going back there was as painful as going to a bull riding, with memories everywhere.

"It's hot. July in Louisiana. Mawmaw is canning okra."

"Oh... I don't suppose she'd send me a jar?" She loved pickled okra and the stuff at the Brookshire Brothers wasn't the same as homemade.

"She'll send you that and some chow chow too."

"That would be a blessing, thank you. I'll send her some nice yarn." She had some lovely alpaca she'd found at a garage sale that would make a nice gift for Beau's mawmaw. The old lady knitted and crocheted blankets and hats for the babies at the hospitals and for the hurricane shelters, as well.

They made it inside the restaurant, and it took forever for the hostess to seat them, but the waitress was with them so fast that they barely had time to talk.

"She'd love that, all right," Beau finally said about Mawmaw, she thought. "Man, I could eat one of everything. Sammy'll be jealous. He loves this place."

She wondered if Les would like it here. Somehow she doubted it. He seemed like he'd want something less fancy. All those beers to choose from. Of course, Beau made good money. Les was like her — working for pennies, so he could eat a lot of ninety-nine-cent corny dogs for what this place cost.

They ordered iced tea and appetizers, and she was glad to see Beau skipping the beer since he was driving.

The artichoke dip was so good, though, and the pasta was real nice when it came, full of tomatoes and cheese and basil.

"You're a million miles away, Rosarita," Beau teased her once he'd powered through a calzone, some garlic bread, and a huge salad.

"Yeah, it's been...different." Everyone had been so kind, and she wouldn't have met Les if she hadn't come, but life was strange. She'd almost kissed him last night, almost did it, but... He hadn't made the first move and she just couldn't figure out how to be that way. She hadn't had a first kiss since she was fifteen and she just wasn't sure how she was supposed to be all 'come take me'.

God, maybe she wasn't ready to date someone new. Maybe she should just give up on this whole fantasy.

"He was a good guy, your Timmy." Beau took her hand, squeezed it, and she nodded.

"He was. I can't believe that it's already been three years. Some days it feels like it was yesterday. Some days it feels like a whole other life ago."

"It takes work to keep going day to day. I feel so damned lucky sometimes, and then sometimes I want to break things." That was a lot of words for Beau, and it said more than he might ever tell anyone but her about Sammy's injuries.

"Yeah." She couldn't imagine living with a broken Timmy. She didn't know how to imagine it. That waylaid madness.

"Sorry about that." He patted her hand before he let go. "You ought to come see us. Make a long weekend out of it sometime soon."

"Don't you be sorry. You know I got your back." And she wouldn't hurt Beau for all the tea in China.

"Thanks." He tried to grin, but that flash of anguish on his face was enough to make Rosie tear up because no one cried alone.

"Hey. Hey, he's okay. He's fine and missing me. See?" Beau grabbed his phone, showing line after line of texts.

The last one just said, "Come home, Boug. I miss you. Next trip, I wanna come."

"Oh." Rosie laughed and if the sound was watery, no one noticed, right? "Good for him. I miss his face."

"So? Say you'll visit." He grinned at her, his air of anticipation clear.

"I will. I'll bring sweets and we'll visit and have a cookout." She did love any excuse to make candy or cookies.

"Make pralines and it's a deal. I'll even leave the gumbo off the menu."

"I want beans and rice with andouille." She loved red beans and rice, and there was always music at Beau and Sam's.

"You got it. Sam will want to do a pig roast." Beau seemed so cheerful at the idea that she had to grin.

"I'm in. I miss the hounds." Drooly, stinky beasts. Droopy too. Nothing like her baby dog. They adored everyone and everything, those monstrous bloodhounds Beau bred. Their ears fascinated her, dangling like minute steaks.

"Oh, God, Boudreaux has taken to being Sammy's balance dog."

"Now, I might pay to see that in person." Boudreaux could get excited and knock a man down.

"See? There you go." He licked sauce off his fork for a moment. "Want to split a big cookie?"

"God yes." She would love that, all melty yumminess and ice cream.

Chocolate solved a multitude of the world's problems.

Chapter Eight

Les stood with his foot up on the rail, watching the first round of bull riders go down like ducks in a carnival game. Boom. Bang. Ouch. Bulls six so far, cowboys zilch.

He was just awaiting his turn on the broncs, and it would be soon, the way the boys were hitting the dirt in two to three seconds.

Lord have mercy.

He nodded to Norville and Pooter, who were taking the long walk down the arena to watch the ropers. Both headers were on a hunt for a good heeler and Les' money was on Norville stealing Troy Montrose's boy before Pooter could.

"Hey, Les." A cowboy he barely knew came to stand next to him, arms up on the rail, booted foot on the bottom of the fence. Montana, this one was from, he thought. Saddle bronc. "You riding today?"

"I am. I pulled Moaning Leo. You?"

"Humdinger. Good motion on that gelding. You're gonna get your neck jerked around."

"Nothing new there." Shit, he'd started thinking he was getting a little long in the tooth for this game, but he kept showing up. The money he could make in one weekend in Cheyenne came out to more than his salary some years. Good thing he got room and board from his day job.

"No, sir," the feller said.

The bull riding section ended and the riders all started milling about as the horses were loaded into the chutes. Les nodded to—shit, was it Pete? Then he headed through the crowd along the fence toward the chutes.

One of the bullfighters was up on the rails, climbing over and heading right toward him, moving like one of the critters in a Japanese horror movie, limping, but so fast Les took a step back. He reckoned he just needed to get out of the way in case the man needed to pee.

"Howdy, cowboy." The voice was familiar and he strained his brain hunting for a name. He'd seen this one the other night with Rosie. Cooper. That was it.

"Mr. Coop. How do?"

"Good. Good. Aching some, but that's not news." Cooper smiled for him but it was rueful as hell.

"Nope." Hadn't he just said that to Montana Pete? Some things never changed in their world. "Did you need something?"

"Just wanted to say hi and say to be gentle with our Rose, huh? She's not a buckle bunny like some. She don't have a prickle in her and she'll always have us to back her up."

Les' cheeks heated in ways the July sun had nothing to do with. "Oh, now. I like the lady a lot, and I swear, I'm not one for playing."

"Good deal. I'd hate to have to kill you. You seem like a decent enough feller." The words weren't offered over in a joking manner at all. No, sir, Coop was serious as a heart attack.

Good thing Les knew how to cowboy up. He was glad Rosie had such staunch defenders, he really was. "Says a lot about the lady that you're so good to her," Les said.

"She's one of us. Tim was a bit of a dipshit, but golden to the core and God save her, she ain't got people, so…" Coop shrugged. "We're her people now and we aim to help her any way we can."

"I like that." Impulsively he stuck his hand out to shake.

Coop took it, fingers callused and damn near raw. Someone had been having a rough show.

All Les could do was wince, knowing Coop wouldn't appreciate the suggestion of going to sports medicine.

"You'd best get ready to ride, cowboy. I'm taking a break." Coop tipped his hat.

"Have a good night, Mr. Coop." Less nodded and brushed on by needing his head in the game.

"Good ride, cowboy."

He sure hoped so. He needed to earn a little more cash before he had to leave town.

Tonight he had a date with the most beautiful girl in the world.

* * * *

She did her eyes—liner and mascara, sparkly shadow and brows. Then she did the rest of her face before she put on her new blouse—white with the prettiest scattering of clear beads over the front. She added a sparkly silver sequined belt to her new Cruel Girl jeans and put on her good boots.

There. She was ready.

God, was this a date?

It was crazy to call it a date even if it was. She was going home soon, and she would probably never see Les again after this one trip. But he sure was cute and sweet and kind, and he was taking her dancing after, so it had to qualify as a real date, right? Not just "let's meet at the rodeo".

Whatever. She wasn't going to end up sleeping with him and Timmy wouldn't mind if they danced. He used to let her dance with Andy Baxter before they got married, didn't he? After they got hitched, well, Andy hadn't been allowed. She grinned a little, remembering Andy sporting that black eye.

Silly boys.

Rose headed down to the lobby, nodding at the receptionist lady and grinning at the goofy "Welcome Rodeo Fans" decorations everywhere.

Les wasn't in the lobby when she got down there, so she went to peek outside. He liked the air and all.

She saw him across the parking lot, slowly getting out of his truck, still in his rodeo clothes, and those were covered in grossness. She winced, something in her shivering a little bit, then went to help. "Hey, cowboy. Looks like a hard day."

"Hey, Rosie." Les had the grace to look a little shame-faced. "I'm sorry I'm late. Can you give me five to get clean?"

"Sure, you've got a ton of time. The concert doesn't start for an hour." She bit back the questions — what happened? How bad was it? How bad are you hurt? No cowboy wanted a nag.

"Thanks, honey. That big bitch of a mare I pulled in the bareback about did me in. Pardon my French." He let her help him to the elevator. "Back in a jiffy."

"No hurry." She brushed her hands off on his jeans and went to sit, telling herself very firmly that she wasn't going to cry and she wasn't going to worry, because she *wasn't* dating Les because she didn't date cowboys. They were having laughs together, even if she wanted him to kiss her and move the earth.

He came back down five minutes later, dressed in his new jeans and a white shirt. The goo was gone, but that made the bruises lurid by comparison.

Rose stood, went right to him. "Are you sure you're okay? We don't have to go."

"No, no. I'm fine, honey. 'Sides, we're gonna be sitting. I got the tickets so we don't have to be in standing room, huh?" He smiled, bent to kiss her cheek, stiff as a scarecrow.

"You did." She knew that smell — the liniment. Timmy used to say the whole locker room area smelled like that. "The shuttle should be here soon and you can sit and rest."

"Let's go grab a bench."

"Sounds good." She led the way, held the door for him. "Did you need a Coke or something?"

"Oh, that's a good idea." He grinned a little, and at least he still had all his teeth. She was picky that way.

"Okay. Sit here. I'll be right back." She headed to the Coke machine, dug out a couple of dollars, and got him a drink. Her fingers were shaking a little bit, but she ignored them. He was a friend. No stress.

He gave her a warm smile when she came back, reaching for the can with bruised knuckles. "I'm sorry, honey. I sure didn't expect to get busted up."

Rose chuckled, the sound just a little dry. How many thousand times had she heard that? "Nobody ever does but the bullfighters."

"Yeah. I guess that's true." He leaned on her gently when she sat down.

"Is there anything I can do to help?" She hated that he hurt.

"Hmm. You could kiss this one and make it better." Les pointed to his chin.

"Oh, you flirt." Still, she leaned up and kissed his chin, gentle as she could. "Better?"

Oh, man. Lipstick stain. "Whoops."

"Much better. What?" He rubbed his chin. "Oh."

"Sorry." She felt her cheeks flame.

"Why? You're a pretty lady. It's natural for a girl to gussy up." He kissed the corner of her mouth just as the bus pulled into the parking lot.

She stood and reached for him. "God, I hope there's a seat for you. There should be. We're the first stop."

"I'm all right, honey." He got up slow, but he made the steps of the bus okay. "I'm not lettin' this ruin our night."

"Stubborn cowboy." She grabbed his Coke and two dollars from her purse, thankful that the seats were open.

"I am." The little driver took her dollars, and they got seats. She made him slide in so he'd be trapped. No one was going to ask her to stand.

She handed him his Coke, frowning at the way he held himself. "Did they give you something at Sports Medicine?"

"They wrapped me up. Don't you worry on it." He shifted the Coke to his opposite hand and grabbed her fingers with the close one.

"Are you looking forward to the concert?" she asked.

"I am. I like George. You?" He played with her fingers, his calluses rough against her.

"Lord, yes. I love to hear him sing. He's so smooth."

"Do you like beer at a concert, honey? Or should we just share another popcorn?"

"If they gave you pain pills, you don't need a beer, Les. You forget, I was married to one of y'all. Your kidneys will thank me. We'll have popcorn."

"Okay." His cheeks went red along with his ears, but he laughed, lifting her hand to kiss the back. "You're a smart lady."

"I am." Her fingers brushed his lips. "I'm so sorry you're hurting."

"So am I. I wanted to be a hundred percent tonight." The bus finally lurched into motion, making Les wince.

She hummed, worrying. "It's okay. We'll have fun. Listening to King George is going to be magic."

It was probably a good thing that they weren't going to dance because he was hurt. She might fall in love if it was good.

"It will." Laughing, he squeezed her hand. "You're something else, lady."

"Just a girl." She grinned over at him, held on, and reminded herself, very firmly.

She didn't date cowboys.

Chapter Nine

Les thought his butt might just fall off.

The George concert had been a fine thing. Watching the way Rosie lit up when that old Texan sang was half the fun. The other half was humming along. The honky tonk, part? Well, it wasn't so great. He'd been willing to try dancing with Rose. His groin pull wasn't. So they was sittin' and having Cokes and curly fries before heading back to the hotel.

Rose didn't complain a bit, though. Hell, she was the one who'd played fetch and carry on their second round of Cokes.

She was a champion among women. Pretty, smart enough to keep him on his toes, and with a built-in knowledge of cowboys. Too bad she was leaving. Like tomorrow.

"You ought to stay on a few more days," he told her, as if wishing would make it so.

"I wish I could, but I have to get back. I have to be at work Monday morning." She stuck out her tongue and rolled her long ponytail around and around, fastening it into a bun. He wanted to know what it looked like, down and loose.

"Shame. I could run you over to Steamboat, let you see a moose or two."

"Tempter." Rose shook her head. "I don't have any paid time, though, and payday is coming quick."

"Well, the offer stands." Just because he was having trouble standing didn't mean he couldn't offer.

"Thanks, cowboy." She patted his hand, gentle as could be.

"Good Lord, Les! I sure didn't expect to see you here tonight!" Rowdy and Rusty came wandering up, both with beers in their hands. The twin team ropers looked like carbon copies of each other, all dark skin and wide, crookedy smiles.

"Hey, boys. I was taking the lady to the concert." He made a show of politely rising half out of chair before sinking back down. "Miss Rose, this is Rowdy, and that's Rusty."

"Pleased." Two Stetson brims went down, then up.

Rose smiled at them. "Would y'all like to sit?"

"Surely." Rusty plopped down, grinned at him. "Shit, man. We thought you were a goner today when that bronc dragged you."

Rowdy nodded. "You know it. Scared us some, laying still on the dirt like that. I thought the worst for a second."

"I'm fine." Les said it between gritted teeth. Damn it, Rose didn't need to hear all that about him getting his chickens scattered.

"Well, good. We'd hate to lose you, man. Hear that you're out for at least a couple weeks."

Rose's eyes were huge, her sweet face milk-pale, and her hand slid away from his, easy as can be. "I need to hit the ladies' room. If y'all will pardon me?"

"Sure, honey." Les waited until she was out of earshot before turning on the boys. "She's a widow, you know. Lost her husband right in the arena. Timmy Cutrer. You boys are making my night difficult."

"Oh, man."

"No shit?"

"Sorry, Les."

"We didn't know."

"Yeah." He stared them down, Rowdy first, then Rusty. "Scoot."

"Uh-huh." They stood up together and practically ran away from the table.

It took two songs before Rose came back, her eye makeup wiped away mostly, her eyes bright. "Where'd your friends go, cowboy?"

"They had to take off. Are you all right, honey?" He took her hand when she sat down, wanting to reassure her.

"I am, yeah. You seem like you're wearing down, though. I could get us a cab so you don't have to wait for the shuttle again."

"Oh, honey, that's okay. The cabs will all be so busy. We can go get the bus." Shit, he didn't want her paying for a cab. Unless she was wanting to get rid of him.

"You're sure?"

"I am. It would take hours." Cheyenne was a small town. He squeezed her hand, not ready to let go yet. "You want anything else to eat?"

"You know what I want?"

He shook his head, willing to get her damn near anything just so she wouldn't cry no more.

"Ice cream. It's really loud in here, Les. Can we go have an ice cream?"

She looked about two seconds away from tears.

"You bet, lady." He levered up, making his face very still, and held out a hand to help her out. "Come on. They got some in the marketplace, and it will be quiet by now."

"Yeah? Excellent." She didn't put any weight on his arm, but she held his hand.

The ice cream place was still open, barely, and they got vanilla for him, mint chocolate for her. It felt real good on his mouth.

There were benches in the square, and they sat, eating, staring out at all the traffic, the partiers, the lights. The wind was blowing, nice and chilly. Cheyenne did cool off as soon as the sun went down.

"So did you have a good time on your vacation, Rosie?" He sure had.

"I did, Les. It was wonderful. I didn't expect it to be at all." She sighed, licked her spoon. "I'm glad you offered me a seat on the bus."

"I am, too." More than he could even say. She was gonna slip away from him, though, and it hurt his gut. He wanted to do something crazy, but that just wasn't his style.

"If you ever come to north Texas, I'll take you for barbecue."

"I'll take you up on that, honey. You ever come to Steamboat, I'll take you to this little Italian place." All of the ranch wives loved it, and he knew she liked Italian food.

"You have my word." She glanced at him, her eyes dark as holes burned in a sheet. "I think I'm going to miss you, Mr. Les."

"I know I'm going to miss you, Rosie." He knew it might be his only chance, because once they got back to the hotel, she'd be thinking on packing and putting this all behind her. Les slid an arm around her waist and pulled her up against him, bending to kiss her mouth. Just so he'd know what she felt like.

She opened for him, leg pressing against his hurt one and he jerked, wincing a little. Rose pulled away, hands fluttering. "Oh. Oh, God. I'm sorry."

"Shh. No. No sorries." He pressed a finger to her lips. "It's been an honor making a friend out of you, Rosie."

She nodded. "You know it, cowboy. You're the best." She sniffled a little, stood. "Come on, Les. Let me get you to the hotel. I know you're sore."

"And you have to get moving, huh?" His hands clenched, but he figured it didn't do no good to get all riled up. He'd head back to Steamboat and she'd go to Texas, and that was that.

"I need to before I forget that I'm not going to fall in love with another rodeo cowboy, huh?" She smiled at him, and the look was bittersweet as hell. "Still, I wouldn't trade the last three days for anything. Well, maybe I wouldn't have you hurt."

"I hear that." Les tucked her arm into the crook of his elbow. "I'd take it again for you, though." They headed off for the bus, chatting about this and that, laughing about the concert and how George had forgot the words.

He knew when they got to the hotel they'd just walk away.

They'd already said goodbye.

Chapter Ten

"So? You made it, huh? Home now?"

Rose nodded, picking up the toys that Presley had strewn around the house during her day at work. "I did. It was a nice memorial, June. You'd have liked it."

She could hear Timmy's momma chuckle, the sound dry and husky. "I doubt it."

"Well, okay, but it was nice. Beau said nice things." And she'd met a cowboy who she couldn't stop thinking about. Les was always in her mind.

"That's good. Mr. Lafitte was always dear." June sighed. "Are you doing okay? Did you manage to have any fun at all, baby girl?"

"I did." The best time in years. She hurt when she thought about it, though.

"Did you meet anyone?"

"June!" Jesus! She checked herself out in the mirror. Did she look...like an unfaithful widow or something?

"What? Robbie, Timmy's been gone for three years. It's time to start getting out there again." June was so practical.

"But... You're his momma, June."

"Yep, and I'll miss him every day until I go to meet him, but he's gone, baby girl."

Like she didn't know that. She knew that. She just… "I don't think…" What? What could she say that wasn't awful?

"Robbie. I love you like you were my own, but you're young. You deserve babies and happiness and to get out of that shitty little apartment."

"It's not that bad."

June snorted. "Right. So? Who is he?"

"Who?" *Oh, God.*

"The cowboy. There was one. I know it. 'Fess up."

June knew her too well now for her to get out of this unscathed. She might as well own up to it.

"His name's Les."

* * * *

Les was taking his sister to lunch in downtown Steamboat.

Lord. That was always a joy and a curse. Hester Anne never wanted to go to the café. She wanted to go to that Italian place on the main drag, the one that made you wait forever for a table, then made you wait some more.

He figured she did it on purpose, just to make him pay for calling her Hes her whole life. Like he liked being Lester any better.

"Hey you." She bustled up to him outside the restaurant to kiss his cheek. She looked good. Smiling, her blue eyes dancing. That was a good sign.

"Hey, lady. How's it going?" He hugged her before wiping the Chapstick off his cheek. Like a lot of Colorado women, Hester Anne was low maintenance in the looks department, but she surely hated dry lips.

"Good. You already put in for a table?"

"Yes, ma'am." Summer season was as busy if not more so than ski season, so he'd gotten there right early.

"How did that last ride in Cheyenne go? You didn't call or text me back, so I assumed you fell off."

"Ha ha. Got third in a go-round the second ride. Got stomped and dragged once."

They got inside and the fluttery little waiter dude seated them before Hes answered. She pursed her lips and tilted her head, and Les braced for whatever she was about to ask.

"You seem happy for third and stomped. What else happened?" she asked.

"Well, I'm going to Texas in about two weeks."

"Texas!" Hes stared, blue eyes narrowing. "You can't have a better job down there."

"Just finishing out the Texas circuit, is all."

"Uh-huh. Spit it out, Lester."

Les took a deep breath. "Well, Hester Anne, I met me a girl."

She chuckled, relaxing back in her chair. "Oh, Lord. Look at you. I swear, you're like a teenager in heat."

"Now, Hes, I haven't been that young in a long time."

"I know it, but she obviously makes you feel like a kid again. Was it good?"

"Hester Anne," Les snapped. "She's a fine lady and I won't talk no trash." There wasn't trash to talk, but Les never had been a kiss and tell type. Not even as a teen.

Hes tilted her head, pursing her lips while she stared. "Okay, then. Tell me who rode won the barrels at the big show." She'd barrel raced in the junior leagues before she got all married and shit.

So instead of giving up Rosie, who he wasn't ready to share yet, he told Hes about the rodeo and their friends around the country and everything but his own life.

That would have to wait until he figured out what he wanted and how to get it.

* * * *

"You know, you can't still be PMSing." Her best friend Lindsay whacked Rose with her big pregnant belly, then winked, pushed all that curly red hair out of her face.

"What?"

"You're scowling again. You're supposed to be asking me about what I want for lunch and whether or not we need to go get pedicures and massages."

Rose sighed, rolled her eyes. "Like I'd want to spend time with you, dork."

Lindsay grinned. "You don't spend time with anyone else." She plopped down into a chair, then reached for Rose's hand. "So? What's up? Was it really terrible? Wyoming?"

"Huh? What? No. No, it was…"

Kind of magical, really, up to the end.

Really.

Lindsay blinked at her, eyes curious. "It was…awful? Cold? Hellish? A blast."

"Neat. It was very neat." And it was very over and no matter what she tried, she couldn't get over it. She'd even called Les twice—once to say thank you for being so nice to her and once to make sure he felt okay. She hadn't talked to him, but on the second call, his voice mail had changed, saying that he was having connection problems, but was missing Texas, which had to be her, right? Because he wasn't in Texas and he wasn't riding in Texas, because she might have had Belle over in reference pull the day sheets for any Texas circuit rodeos so she could search for his name.

Still…

"Rose?"

"What?"

"What's his name, honey?" Lindsay squeezed her fingers, grinned. Silly woman knew her too well.

"Les. Les Jacoby."

"Yeah?" Lindsay leaned her elbows on the table. "Tell."

"Yeah. He was…" Wow. And also, hell yes.

"Great in bed?"

"Linds! We didn't even kiss!" Not really.

"Why not?" Now Lindsay seemed shocked. Of course she did. She always said she didn't buy a pair of shoes without trying them on.

Rose rolled her eyes. "I'm married."

"Widowed."

"Careful." She frowned. Okay, so she used that as an excuse, but she had to have one.

"Scared." Lindsay snorted. "I want to know everything—every detail."

"Nosy old cow." Rose started giggling as that crotchety woman from the front desk, Arlene, sniffed at them disapprovingly.

"Moo…" Her best friend shook her head. "No, really. I want to know everything over pedicures. Then you can plan my baby shower over massages."

Rose rolled her eyes like thrown dice, this close to cracking up. "You've had two baby showers already!"

"Absolutely, so this one has to be *spectacular!*" Lindsay tugged her up. "Come on, my treat. Let's go be ladies who lunch."

Rose nodded, grabbed her purse. Lord have mercy, Lindsay could make a scene. Better get her out of the library.

She wondered if Les liked pink toenails.

* * * *

The truck was packed. He'd talked to the boss one more time, just to make sure his job would still be there come fall, just like always.

"You sure you want to go gallivanting off after this girl?" Harris had asked, sitting at his desk in the big house and squinting at Les over his little wire glasses.

Les had only smiled and nodded, shifting from foot to foot. "Yes, sir. I hope to bring her back with me in the fall."

"Well…" The old man had sniffed. "We could use a woman's touch around here. Maybe we'll get you one of the houses cleaned up."

Oh, that would be something. "I would love that, sir. I really would. Now, I can't take Iggy with me. Do you think Chester would take him again?"

"That man would take Iggy full-time."

"No way." They'd chuckled, but Les had sure been relieved.

So Iggy was provided for, he'd gotten two part-time kids to do most of his work, and he'd lined him up a place to stay down near Rosie so he could ride the circuit and be close enough to see her most days.

That was assuming she wanted to see him. He hadn't actually gotten to talk to her. He'd been up in the high pastures since Cheyenne, moving stock. No one's cell worked up there, just the two-way. She'd left him messages, though, and that had given him hope.

He checked his bag one more time, then gave up on dithering and climbed up in the truck, heading south. Might as well give it a go. If his Rosie girl wanted him as much as he wanted her, well, it would be worth all the trouble.

If she didn't... Hell, a cowboy needed to know. He couldn't live his life on what-ifs, now could he?

Chapter Eleven

"Presley, stop jumping, you little *dork*." Rose grabbed a Beggin' Strip, held it up. "Sit."

Bright little black button eyes stared at her and Presley barked, one paw flailing in the air.

"No. You sit and you can have it. Then it's time for *No Reservations* and *Under a Tuscan Sun*. I have popcorn — I have a glass of wine. I'm ready."

She even had her softest short shorts, the most comfy tank, and her good scrunchie in her hair.

Presley looked, barked, then sat.

"Good dog." Rosie gave Presley his treat and he ran off to eat it in his bed.

She grabbed the wine and the bowl, then headed for her baby sofa. Kleenex? Check. Blanket in case the air conditioning got too cold? Check. Chocolate ice cream in the freezer when the crying over the movie turned into crying over some boy?

Check.

Häagen-Dazs level, check.

Knock at the door and Presley going nuts? Damn it.

"Just a second!" She grabbed Pres, tucked him under her arm and gently popped his nose before unlocking the deadbolt. "No barking. That's rude. Can I help...?"

Oh. Wow. Rosie stopped dead, her mouth falling open.

Les Jacoby stood right there in the hallway, a summer straw on his head, which was odd, because it was Texas-shaped. No. Texas cowboy hat shaped, not like the state.

"Les!" She grinned, bouncing a little, which made Presley peep. "Is it really you? I can't believe it. Come in. Good night, you seem like you feel better."

Oh, God. Les. As in, gee, I'm trouble for a gal in Wranglers Les. At her door.

"Thanks." He smiled, doffing his hat, his eye lines crinkling hard. "You look real pretty. This must be Presley, huh?"

"Pretty? God. I look like a schlub. Sit. Would you like... Well, I have tea and wine. No beer. And yes, that's Presley. Presley, stop, huh. Get down."

"Tea would be fine. It's hot as the hubs of Hades here." He grinned and set his hat where Presley couldn't get it. He sat easily, no popping or cracking or wincing.

"Sure." She grabbed a tumbler out of the cabinet and filled it with ice and tea. God, she didn't have on a bit of makeup.

Or a bra.

When she came back, Presley was sitting on Les' lap, panting happily while strong fingers dug into white fur. Slut dog.

"If he's bothering you..." She handed the tea over, pushed her ponytail off her face.

"Not a bit. Been missing my Iggy anyway." Les sipped, tan throat working. "So how have you been?"

She sat in the wee chair, cross-legged, smiling at him. "Hot, mostly. Working a little. You?"

"Well, I came down to ride some. Season is a bit longer down here."

"Oh? So... You're just passing through?" That was...disappointing. To just have him for a few hours instead of days like last time.

Wait.

Stop.

No having.

"Well, not exactly." Les' cheeks went red as anything. "I, uh, found me a place to stay with some boys here in Longview, so I can sorta base my operation here for a month, at least."

"A month? Oh, that's nice news!" She grinned so hard her cheeks hurt. "I mean, we could have supper and visit."

"We could." The corners of his mouth pulled into a wide smile. "I was sure hoping you'd want to."

"I told you, there's an amazing barbecue place, and that's just the start."

Presley was in love, Rose could tell. The dog had hopped off Les' lap and was bringing him toys.

The red ball.

The blue squeaky bone.

The earless cat.

All three rubber chickens.

Her best panties.

"Presley!"

"Oops." Les chuckled, politely grabbing the ball to toss while she disposed of the undies.

God, how embarrassing! She shoved the panties as deep into the hamper as they'd go, and tried to decide whether she'd be less conspicuous putting on an overshirt now or just dealing with the fact that she was braless.

"You okay, honey?" Les sounded like he might have gotten up to check on her, his voice closer than she expected.

"Yeah. Yeah." She decided to go without, headed back into the front room. "I was sorta stunned at how...messy I look."

"I think you look real fine." His eyes slid over her, the smile she got appreciative without being weird.

"You're a sweetie, but, wow." She smoothed her shirt over her belly. "Have you had supper already?"

"Nope. I was hoping you'd want to have some with me."

"I was planning microwave popcorn and ice cream and chick flicks. Supper sounds way more fun." She grinned at him. "Give me ten minutes to get presentable?"

"You bet." He clucked, and Presley hopped right up in his lap again, wagging like mad.

"Okay. Here's the remote." Boys liked remotes and, although she hadn't kept Timmy's big screen, her TV was okay.

"Thanks." The channels started to change like clockwork. Boys...

Okay. Okay. Pink sundress? Too fancy. Jeans and T-shirt? Too casual. Heels? Flip-flops? Boots?

She headed into the bathroom to do her hair and eyes. Maybe her little peasant blouse from the Cato's with a pair of capris and sandals...

Chapter Twelve

Les waited, holding that ridiculous little excuse of a dog on his lap and grinning like a fool.

She'd been happy to see him. Tickled. Jesus, he was so relieved he thought he might bust. He'd put all his cards on the table and bet everything he had on this trip. It was good to know it might just work.

He searched around her tiny apartment, shook his head. It was a little like peeking into a dollhouse, really, with pink and flowers and lace and romance books. There was a huge basket of yarn beside the couch, along with a pile of *Cosmopolitan* magazines. On the coffee table, there was a glass of red wine, a bowl of popcorn, a box of Kleenex, and a stack of movies with kissing folks on the covers.

Lord.

You couldn't tell she'd ever been married to a bull rider — that was for sure. She needed a man around the place.

The only sign that there'd ever been a husband was in the framed pictures on the mantle. There were a couple of little kids, a couple of old folks, and Timmy

Cutrer on his wedding day, sporting one hell of a black eye and stitches on his lip.

Look at that. Les glanced around before letting the grin come. Kid had been good. Les remembered that much about him.

"Sorry. My hair was a huge tangle." Rosie came out of the bedroom — which was a wash of pink and purple flowers, Lord help him — in a blue shirt and a wee pair of short pants, fresh as a daisy.

She had cowhide flip-flops on, with sparkly things on the toes. Pink toenails. That made him grin. Oh, she was a picture. "Not a problem, honey. My sister says a man should be plumb grateful for any time a woman spends making the world a more beautiful place."

Oh, look at her blush and smile. "Flatterer. Presley, come on, baby boy. In the crate."

The little critter yipped and bounced right in, and she tossed in a ball and a treat.

"Oh, man, that's good, honey. Iggy fights me every inch." 'Course Iggy just stayed outside when Les went away during the day. He went to Hester Anne's when Les was gone-gone, and stayed at the ranch when Les went to Texas. Which had just now happened.

"What kind of dog is Iggy, again?" She grabbed a white purse and her keys.

"He's a mix. Mostly hairy. Huge." Les grinned, pulling out his phone. "Here. Here's a picture."

She leaned against his arm, peeking. "Oh, he's beautiful."

"He's a big dork." She felt so good against him. So soft.

"He has pretty eyes." Her fingers stroked his wrist. "What kind of food do you want?"

"Well, you said something about barbecue, but I'm easy." He would eat just about anything.

"The Pit it is." She pointed to a teeny little bright yellow Toyota pickup. "That one's mine. I think you'll fit…"

"Would you rather take my truck, honey? It's in the visitor parking." He would fit in it so much better.

"You sure? I'm just thinking you've got those long, long legs…"

"I don't mind a bit. You just tell me which way to turn." The small truck might have meant snuggling, but his hat would end up crushed against the headliner.

"That's easy. It's just right off the Interstate."

"Cool." He got her in the truck, which he'd had detailed that morning to get rid of the three day drive smell.

She looked so pretty, sitting in his truck. She pointed the way, then her laugh filled the cab. "I can't believe you're here, Les."

"Yeah?" Was that good or bad? In the 'I never once thought of you' way, it could be bad.

"Well, an hour ago I was going to spend the evening on the sofa crying with Sandra Bullock and now you're *here*."

"I am. I, uh, might have picked here for the rest of the summer 'cause of you." There. It was out. She'd find out anyway.

"Oh…" Those dark eyes flashed up at him. "You know, I said I wasn't going to date cowboys, right? So this isn't a date."

"Nope. This is two friends going to have barbecue." He wasn't gonna push. But like Hester had said, he only lived once and he'd never mooned over a girl before. Not only that, he wasn't interested in dating. He wanted forever and that happy smile, well, it gave him hope.

He smelled the barbecue before he saw the building, but man, he could remember why Texas was so cool, smelling that. Yum. "This place has to be a winner, honey."

"It's so good, here. The beans are real hot, though."

"Oh, good to know." The place with crowded with pickups and SUVs, and Les wondered idly how many people would know Rosie.

She walked in with him and although everyone was nice, nobody seemed to recognize her at all. Weird. Of course, maybe he was just so small town that he was used to everyone being all up in his business. He held her hand while she swung her leg over the bench before plopping down next to her.

"I haven't been here in years. It still smells so good."

Ah. Well, that explained why no one had her number. "What do you like best?"

"The brisket sandwich and a side of coleslaw. Timmy used to say that their ribs were good, but I don't like them much."

"I might have to have the three meat plate, then." Brisket, ribs and sausage.

The waitress came over. "Evenin'. Do y'all want tea, Coke or beer?"

"Tea, for me, please." Les smiled, betting she would take tea, too, but not willing to order for her yet.

"Me, too." Rosie nodded happily, her long ponytail bobbing behind her.

"Sure. Here's some bread." The waitress left them, and Les shook his head.

"White bread. Lord." That always cracked him up. Colorado barbecue owed a lot to Texas, but the bread had more body to it.

Rosie giggled, patted his leg. "Welcome to Texas, cowboy."

"Yeah. At least this has sesame dealies." There was one place that just gave you a half a loaf of white bread, still in the bag. Roadside barbecue, that place.

"So what do they serve with barbecue where you're from?"

"Oh, the places up my way usually do crusty French stuff. Or cornbread."

"Mmm. Cornbread." She didn't sweeten her tea. He sort of filed that away, too. It was a little creepy, how he wanted to know all this stuff. Was he getting all stalkery? Shit, he hoped not. Les munched some bread with sauce, just to shut up his brain. "So, what have you been doing, the last few weeks?" she asked.

Looked like he wasn't the only one who wanted to know stuff. His brain stood up to cheer, but he played it cool.

"Well, I took a week off or so, just to get over that groin pull. Then I did a couple small rodeos before I went back to the ranch and squared things with my boss to come here." He didn't have to be back until two weeks after Labor Day.

"Was he upset that you came?"

"Nope. He just wanted to make sure I'd be back for winter this year. It'd leave him in the lurch if I didn't go move stock to winter pasture." He wouldn't do that to old man Harris.

"That would suck, huh? I've just been working."

"Well, I'll be about a bit, if you want to go out and cut a rug or some such. We never got to dance in Cheyenne."

"I'd love that. I work normal office hours — three days at the city, two at the library."

"Well, there you go. I'd love it, too." He loved it so much that he was hanging out in a trailer house with six early twenty-something to late teen bull riders, putting his sleeping bag out on their screened porch. Least it had a fan and not too many bugs.

He moved the beans side of the plate closer to her. Seemed like she liked spicy. He'd remember that. She was from Louisiana, she'd told him at the Village Inn, sprinkling hot sauce on her eggs.

They chatted while they ate, and it was just like before—solid and easy, and he felt like she enjoyed listening to him, gave a shit what he had to say. She was so pretty too. He could watch her forever, just jones on the way her mouth moved, the way her hair smelled.

"Is my lipstick messed up, Les?" Rosie dabbed her mouth.

"Huh?" Oh, shit, was he staring? "No, honey. It's fine."

"You sure?" She winked at him. "This makeup stuff is way more work than the television lets on."

"I'm sure. You look perfect." He thought she was beautiful without the makeup.

He watched that sweet face turn pink, from her lips to her dark hair. "Thank you."

"You're welcome." Les let his fingers brush over hers again, because he could.

Her fingers curled with his, squeezed, just for a second.

Les smiled, letting that be enough for now. He had beans and brisket, and the prettiest girl ever sitting next to him. He just had to stay in the saddle between now and the whistle.

Chapter Thirteen

"And the big bad wolf said, 'I'll huff, and I'll puff, and I'll blo-o-o-o-ow your house down!'" Rose grinned as the three and four year olds laughed, clapping as she read. Preschool story time made her happy. Summer reading club was sort of a special thing, from beginning to end.

She had drawn a million piggies, had bounced around the library like a kangaroo, and had become a master of monkey noises.

She was having a ball.

The kids were, too, she could tell. There was a towheaded pair of twins who made her biological clock tick, and they loved the big bad wolf. A lot. She finished the book, they sang the circle song, then she got her hugs and kisses. By the time everyone had been delivered to their folks, she was ready to get off work and go have supper and a movie with her cowboy.

Who was standing just outside the children's area, hat in his hand, smiling at her with his white teeth and bright blue eyes. *Beautiful man.*

"Oh, look at you smile." Lindsay nudged her, took the box of supplies from her with a wicked grin. "Go. Have fun. Return Tuesday with tales of naughtiness that will fuel my dreams."

"Linds!"

"Go, girlfriend. You. Me. Lunch. Tuesday."

She nodded, chuckled and waved to Les. "Come meet my friend, cowboy."

Les nodded easily, walking over, his long old legs seeming to move slow but eating up the space. He smiled at Lindsey, who fluttered a bit. "Ma'am."

"Lindsay, Les. Les, Lindsay." She chuckled under her breath as her increasingly pregnant friend blushed and fluttered.

"Pleased to meet you. You mind me being nosy? Is it a boy or a girl?"

"It's a boy." Lindsay's hand rubbed over her belly. "James Marcus."

Rose grinned, pleased that the usual jealous pang hadn't come this time. "This is number three for her and Frankie."

"Number three. Well, congratulations." Les shook Lindsay's hand, just sweet as pie, before turning to her. "You ready, Rosie?"

"Yes, sir." She grabbed her purse from behind her desk, made sure her blouse was passable.

He offered his arm, letting her rest her hand in the crook of his elbow. "So, what movie are we gonna see tonight, honey?"

"Nothing sad. You have a choice between explosions and gunfights."

"Gunfights, huh?" He gave her a sideways glance. "Which one is grosser?" He'd been around a few weeks, now. He knew she didn't like a lot of gore.

"The cop one seems like it's a little nasty. The other one's like a spaceship thing, so more monsters." Lord, it was warm outside.

"Spaceships it is." Poor Les had to be melting. He'd told her it hardly ever got higher than eighty where he lived.

"Come on. Let's eat. It's deadly out here today." She led him into Pecina's, sat him down.

"Thanks. I could use some iced tea, for sure." His hat came off again. His momma had raised him right.

"Poor mountain cowboy. Don't you melt away, now. You leave that to Frosty the Snowman." She waved to the waitress and got them a couple of teas. "How was your day? I didn't expect you to pick me up at the library."

"Oh, I had to be downtown anyway, had to go to the Western Union. Mom's debit card got canceled again." Les chuckled. "They're traveling fools."

"Oh, man. How scary! Are they still in Mexico?"

"Yeah. Somewhere by the seashore." He reached over, touching her fingers. He was a hand-holder, her Les. Except he wasn't hers. No, sir. Because she didn't get serious cowboys.

She did hold hands with them, though. "So, do you want enchiladas today or burritos?"

"I think enchiladas. I do love the gravy stuff. Oh! Or them avocado ones." She'd found out that as far as Les was concerned, enchiladas came with green chile. He'd been exploring his options every time they went out.

She laughed and nodded. "I want a fajita taco. One of the babies at story time must have had them for lunch. I've been smelling fajitas all day."

"Well, there you go. Need to get that out of your system. Then maybe some sopapillas." The man had an unnatural fascination with fried bread. It was cute.

"You're going to make me fat." She chuckled, leaned against him for half a second.

"Uh-huh. I'm not sure that's possible, honey."

"Well, maybe." She winked, settled back when the waitress brought the chips.

"Maybe." He tilted his head like a dog hearing a whistle. "Why didn't you have kids?"

"What?" She grinned, blinked. That had come out of nowhere.

"You and Timmy. Why didn't you have kids?" His ears were on fire, but he carried on, bless him. "I saw you at the library. You love them."

"I do. We both did. I..." She chewed on her bottom lip. "We just didn't ever catch and I. Well, I went to the lady doctor and... Well, all my tests were good, so— Well, Timmy thought we'd just wait and see if it happened."

Because her cowboy wasn't going to jerk off into some cup or anything. Not ever.

"Ah." Les nodded sagely. "Yeah, I can see that." He gave her a gentle smile.

Oh. Oh, good. Okay. Yay. He understood. Heck, it was a common problem among roughstock riders, right?

She really didn't want to have to explain more.

"Do you like babies?" Cowboys tended to like them, tended to want them. Not that she cared because she wasn't dating and if she was dating, it wouldn't be a cowboy...

"I do. I mean, I have a couple of nephews, and I've always been good with them." If his ears went redder, they might've burst into flames.

"Oh, that's neat. I mean, kids are..." She glanced at Les, then they both started laughing. "We're great big dorks."

"We are. Look, *queso*." They started in on the cheese dip, and talk turned back to movies and stuff.

Every so often their eyes would meet, though, and his expression would sort of…burn. He watched her eat too. Like when she'd bet he thought she wasn't noticing. His gaze settled on her mouth a lot.

By the end of dinner, she was shivering just a little, her nipples hard as rocks. She might not get serious about cowboys, but she sure wanted this one.

Les picked up the bill, which he'd been doing a lot of, and helped her up when they were ready to head out. He'd gotten all cowboy on her the one time she argued hard about going Dutch.

"You know… We could go back to my place and just watch a movie, if you wanted…"

"Yeah? I'd like that." Les led her to the truck, the heat waves battering at them.

"Me too. I have popcorn, I bought the beer you like, and we can relax." Wait. Was that a come-on? Was that cool? She felt psycho, wavering back and forth between ready for action and scared to death.

"Sure, honey." His hand lingered on her waist when he helped her up in the truck, but he wasn't smarmy or anything.

Rose caught herself fluttering, and she looked over at Les, reached for his hand where it sat on the seat between them. "I'm all bouncy tonight."

"I don't mind a bit, honey." He gave her this little sideways glance, mouth kicking up, and it made her flutter some more.

"You…" She fanned herself a little bit. "Lord have mercy, it's warm out today." And she was being hormonal and psycho.

"It is melty." He turned the air up for a little.

Alan Jackson came on the radio and she hummed along, swaying side to side. Les chuckled, making the turn on the highway that would take them back to her place. He was learning his way around pretty good.

"Are you laughing at me, cowboy?" She dared to stretch over again, touch his thigh playfully.

"No, ma'am. I'm enjoying you singing." He reached down and squeezed her hand.

She let her fingers twine with his, thumb rubbing a scar on his hand. "This from roping?"

"Yep. Not rodeoin', though. There was this rogue calf and an impending late-season blizzard." His fingers felt fine against hers.

"Was the calf okay?" Poor hand. Ropes could be vicious, but what those boys could do was fascinating.

"Yeah. He made it through." Les seemed so pleased that it made her laugh.

"We had cattle when Timmy was alive — twenty of them. They were neat."

"Yeah? Did he throw calf nuts at you?" Something about Les' expression told her he'd done that.

She giggled, winked. "Only the once. I did a lot of the work with them, because he traveled."

"So you can work cattle?" Now that look was pure admiration. "Go you, honey."

"I can. Don't tell anyone, but Timmy couldn't ride a horse, so I did. He did his stuff on the four-wheeler."

"No shit? Well, I guess some guys can't. I've seen it at rodeos, fellers who can't do their victory lap." They turned into her lot, and Les slid his monster of a truck right into the visitor's spot.

"Yeah, it's different — sport versus cowboying."

"Yep. Got to admit that's why I never went to bull riding full-time." Those wide shoulders moved in a shrug. "Smaller rodeos are kinder to cowboys like me."

"Yeah. It… It's not fun so much, being the wife in the big show. They like the boys to be available so the women come watch and get autographs signed."

"Yeah? Well, I guess I can see that. That'd make me crazy, it was the other way around, though." He helped her out of the truck, hand on her bare arm, right up next to her breast.

She smiled, leaned into him a little. "Yeah. I guess you've seen the boys tear it up 'cause somebody danced with somebody else's gal or something."

"Hell, yes. My sister's husband, 'fore he was, you know. He would try to tear the head off anyone who cast eyes on her."

"There you go. I used to dance with Andy Baxter all the time, till me and Timmy got married. Then he wouldn't have it." It was how it worked.

"Well, no. I'd expect you to— Oh! Oh, honey, that's what we ought to do." Les swung her back around and headed right for the truck.

"Les?" She laughed, following along.

"We're going dancing, honey." He twirled her in a little do-si-do. "I owe you one, you know?

"Oh. Oh, are you sure?" Oh, God. She… She loved dancing and she hadn't in so long and…

Yeah. Wow.

Of course, he was tall and she wasn't. They probably wouldn't fit together at all. It would probably be a disaster. Then she'd know, right? She'd know that they weren't meant to be together.

"I really do. You just point me toward the honky tonk." He helped her back into the truck, giving her some serious déjà vu.

"Uh… The Ranch House has a sweet little dance floor and a band on Thursday." She pointed down the interstate.

"Then we'll head there, have a beer." He gave her a little smile. "Or a glass of wine. Scoot our boots."

"For real? I mean, you don't have to…" But, man, she hoped he wanted to.

"For real, honey. I like to dance with a pretty girl." That made her blush, duck her head, and smile. They busted on down the highway to the Ranch House, and Les let out an appreciative whistle when they pulled in. "Now this is a good place to dance."

"It is. I mean, it used to be. It's been a while." Oh, God. What if *she* sucked at dancing now?

"Well, I might be a little rusty, but I think we'll do all right."

There weren't too many trucks in the lot yet, so maybe she wouldn't embarrass herself.

"We'll be fine." They headed in to the bar and Les paid their cover. Sometimes it was good to be the girl.

"We will. Let's get that little table over there, huh? What do you want to drink, honey?" Les held her chair. It was the little things he did automatically that made him so amazing.

"I think I'd like a Bud Light, please."

"Be right back." Bending, he kissed her cheek, making it very clear who she was there with to any of the cowboys who might be watching.

She smoothed her hair, made sure her shirt was okay.

Les came back with a Bud Light and a Coors. She gave him no end of teasing about his Colorado beer. "There now. Band starts in fifteen minutes. I made sure they were good for two-steppin'."

"Oh, neat." She didn't bounce. She didn't. Because she didn't fall in love with cowboys anymore and she'd never fallen in love with one who danced and Les was tall and it probably wouldn't work. There went the crazy voice in her head again.

"Yep. Good thing we ate, though, else I'd be ordering one of everything fried." Les winked before settling next to her. The man positively never sat across from her. He said he wanted to be close enough to hold hands.

"I used to love their onion rings." She sipped her beer, humming at the cold when it hit her belly.

"We may have to get some later, just to keep our strength up." The band got up on the stage, doing a little tuning.

"That would be fun. They have ranch dip." Her feet were already tapping and the beer made her feel warm.

"I like that. I like the ranch stuff with the chiles too." Les had taken a liking to the chipotle ranch stuff. That man could eat.

"I bought the stuff to make you homemade gumbo." She grinned, winked. "Don't worry, it's not Beau's recipe — it's my mom's."

He gave her a little bit of a blank look, but smiled and nodded. "I like gumbo."

"Mmm. I do too. We'll have that and cornbread. You just tell me when is good for you." She had the stuff for caramels, too, but that was a surprise.

"Well, I got no plans to ride this Sunday." He nudged her leg with his, real gentle.

"It's a date, then." She let herself rub back, her toes curling a little.

The band finally started up, and she figured they'd sit a bit, because no one else was out there dancing. She was wrong. Les got right up and offered his hand.

"Come on, Rosie. Let's cut a rug."

"Surely." She took his hand, reminding herself that this wasn't going to work. It was going to be like a sign from God.

He led her out on the dance floor, turning her to face him. He took her hand and her waist and off they went, starting off with a nice, slow waltz.

Oh.

Oh, damn.

She used to dream about dancing with a boy when she was little, and she'd danced with a lot of cowboys since then and had loved it. It hadn't ever been better than she'd imagined, though. Les held her like a man who knew what he was doing, a man who liked to dance. She fit right up against his breastbone, kinda, and it should have been bumpy. It wasn't.

Rose closed her eyes and let him lead her around. She could hear his heart beating, sweet and soft, right in her ear. His chest vibrated when he hummed with the music, and before she knew it, the tempo changed. Les stepped out smartly to the two-step, really giving her a go.

God was either the meanest thing ever, or loved her more than she deserved, because she wasn't ever dating a cowboy ever again, but she sure as shit was falling in love with one. Strong arms held her close, long legs ate up the floor, and she felt like she was floating. Oh, he was good.

She blinked up at him as they made a turn, looking up into Les' face. "Magic."

Les laughed, the sound gentle and fond. "You are, Rosie. I swear, you make me happy."

"Are you going to think bad of me, if I ask you back to the apartment, for the night?" They hadn't even kissed, not with high-dollar intent and all, but...well, their bodies felt so nice together and she was a widow, not some green girl.

He stopped dead, right there on the dance floor. "No, Miss Rosie. I am not going to think poorly of you for any reason." It took someone almost knocking into them to get Les moving again.

She let herself lean into him, let herself touch. Let him know that she wanted. His hand slid down her waist to rest on the upper swell of her butt. He was letting her know too. The music slowed and so did the lights, everything going to belt buckle polishing. Rose was in heaven. Les pulled her close, this low growly noise coming out of him. She could feel him, feel what was below his belt buckle, pressing against her. She lifted her face, making the offer. She wanted to know what his kisses tasted like. Les sidestepped them to the side of the floor and bent down, kissing her full on the mouth. His lips were warm, still not too damp, and they fit just right on hers. It wasn't wild, because this wasn't private, but it was slow and sweet, and enough to heat her to the core, make her moan.

Les groaned a little too, pulling back to stare into her eyes. "I'm not sure I can do that much longer and stay polite, honey."

"I think. I think we ought to… Come home with me, cowboy?" Her heart thudded against her ribs.

"Yes, ma'am. You locked your purse in the truck, right?" He steered her toward the door.

"I did." She loved how his hand felt, solid and strong on her side.

"Then we can leave the beers." They sped up some. She didn't need the rest of her beer. She already felt a little high, a little tipsy.

Les helped her into the truck, leaning in to kiss her again before he closed the door. She was vibrating like a strummed E-string, nipples hard, a ball of heat in her belly. Les kept stealing glances at her, kept sneaking in touches. Her leg, her arm, fingers brushing her breast.

All the way home. By the time they parked, she was breathless and flushed, embarrassingly excited.

Les was Mr. Tall and Silent, but she could see it in his eyes, in the way his jaw clenched. He wanted just as bad.

They got upstairs and she locked the door. He put his hat on the hook that she'd put up three weeks ago, just for him. Then they looked at each other and she stepped right up into his arms and let their bodies touch. Les' arms wrapped around her, and he bent to kiss her, this time deep and long. Not real hard, but real exploratory.

His hands slid up her back, the caress making her moan.

"Sweet lady." Les murmured it against her mouth, lips moving on hers. "Sweet."

She hummed, snuggling in. The heat of his chest against her made her moan — the feel of his hardness against her belly was so fine. It was easy to reach up, pull the band out of her hair, let it down. Boys were fascinated by her hair, and she'd seen Les' eyes on it, more than once.

A tiny noise escaped him, and he pushed one hand up into the heavy stuff, tilting her head to kiss her again.

This time the kiss left her breathless, left her clinging to his shoulders. Les moved a tiny bit, and suddenly she was pressed up against his chest, his leg between hers, holding her up on tiptoe. He felt hot, hard and hungry against her.

"Les." She pressed down, the friction making her gasp a little. Oh. Oh, it'd been so long.

"Right here. You feel so good, honey." His hand pressed against her bottom, helping her rub a little.

"Gonna make me embarrass myself." She kissed along his jaw, tongue dragging on his five o'clock shadow.

"Nothing to be embarrassed about, huh? We ain't kids." Les made it sound that simple, as if anything they did together was okay with him. Her practical man.

"No. No, we're not." She hummed, just under her breath. "I haven't done this with anyone but Timmy. You'll have to tell me if I don't do it like you like it."

"Honey, you're doing just fine. Just fine." Les smiled, the expression gentle, fond and real horny around the edges.

"Good." She grinned at him, rubbed their noses together, then kissed him again, like she meant it. His other hand came down, too, squeezing her butt. His body felt good and right against hers, strong and steady. She let one of her hands touch his belly, stroke nice and easy in long motions.

They rocked like they were dancing again, Les humming against her mouth. "We might have to move this to the bedroom, honey."

"I'd like that." She licked his bottom lip, then took his hand and led him into her room. He glanced around, eyebrow arching at the pink flowery everything, and Rose chuckled. "What? I'm a girl."

"You need a man around the place, honey." Les chuckled, turning her to face him fully again, working at her blouse.

"You think?" She grinned at him, then returned the favor, slipping little mother of pearl buttons out of their holes.

"I do. I think you could use some plaid." He chuckled, shrugging out of the shirt when she pushed it down.

"I like plaid." The undershirt went next, right before she lost her blouse. She slid her fingers up Les' belly, a soft moan leaving her at the soft hairs tickling her palms.

"Oh, good." Les unclipped her bra, his little fumble reassuring somehow.

She shrugged out of the delicate lacy thing, trying hard not to worry if she looked okay. If her boobs were big enough, perky enough, pretty enough. Les sure seemed to like them. He stared, and his hands moved up and around, pushing up under her breasts. His hands were so big, the skin rough but warm. Rose pushed up on tiptoe, rocking into the touch. "Les..."

"Soft. You've got sweet skin, Rosie." He kissed the corner of her mouth, then he slid down to her throat.

Her nipples were hard enough that they ached, and her breath sped as his lips headed south, brushing over the swell of her breast. Licking gently, Les worked down to one nipple before closing his mouth around it. He sucked, soft and slow. This deep sound left her, and her head fell back. It was like a line of pleasure, starting from the peak of her nipple and moving through her body, sliding through to the center of her body.

Les made a rough noise, as his mouth moved on her skin, and his tongue came out to taste. His thigh pushed farther between her legs, giving her something to rock against, some sweet friction as her hips rolled in time with the suction at her breast.

It was like dancing all over again, only a whole lot more X-rated. Les wasn't in a hurry, not like Timmy always had been, but it was good. Different good.

Her belly went tight and she was sure he could feel her getting damp.

Les finally just picked her up and carried her the rest of the way to the bed. Didn't strain him even a little.

She settled on the mattress, then carefully worked his buckle open, kisses just barely brushing his belly.

"Rosie." He was so hard for her. She could see it under his jeans, could feel it against her hand when it brushed against his fly.

"You smell good." She loved that, the way a man's body smelled when he was hard, needy.

"You... Oh, honey. I can't talk." He was just moving restlessly, touching whatever part of her he could, his eyes eating her up.

"You're communicating just fine, cowboy." Rose helped him strip down, get his jeans and socks and briefs off. He looked good to her, and she reached out and touched him, stroked him once from base to tip.

"Oh. God." He jerked, his cock swelling in her hand. It was kind of fascinating.

"I..." She kissed the tip, right by the ridge where it flared out, so careful. "This okay?"

"Okay?" He croaked it, his eyes like fire. "Oh, honey, you got no idea how okay that is."

That made her smile, made her rub her thighs together a little, and she kept on exploring. Touching here, tasting there. He let her have her way. His thighs went tense, his balls swayed, and he moaned, his belly like a board. His hands slid into her hair, but he didn't hold her tight or force her or anything. He just petted.

So patient. Rose hummed. She liked this. Not hurrying, it was like a slow dance. You knew the quick ones were coming, but you still had this one, the whole way.

"Come here, honey." He finally tugged her back up, kissing her, not seeming to mind at all that drops of him were still on her lips.

She'd kicked her shoes off, and his hands were warm on her waist, above her jeans.

They kissed, the touches going deep, Les' tongue pushing into her mouth. His fingers got to working on her button, her zipper.

She sucked in to let him in, and that slid her nipples along his chest.

"Oh..." Her eyes rolled and she stepped closer.

"Sweet lady." Les smiled against her mouth, then kissed her again. Then again.

He was sliding her jeans down before she knew it, his hands warm and sure, not nervous at all where they cupped her butt. She arched her back, pushed back into the touch. His skin felt so warm, so good against her. His lips did, too, and they trailed down her neck, leaving a line of fire.

Her skin tingled, everything lit up as he licked.

Les took his time, making her shake. Heck, he made her want to holler at him to speed up.

Of course, once his lips circled her nipple, started sucking in a steady, firm rhythm, she forgave him. Immediately. She held on while he bent her back a little, letting her lower body press against him. Les held her easily, not letting her fall.

"Want you." Sort of like she wanted to breathe.

"I want you, too, honey. We need to get to the horizontal part of the evening." Les backed her up and eased her down.

She didn't know where to put her hands, where to put her eyes.

Then she knew, because he was so fine, taking the last of those clothes off, that she had to explore everything. Just everything.

"Mmm..." This hungry sound came out of her and she licked her lips. He was so fine—strong and solid and real and she wanted to learn every inch.

"This all right, honey?" Les didn't show off or anything, he just paused before he slid into bed next to her, waiting for her nod.

"More than." She pressed close, smiling at how warm he was. "We've been real patient, cowboy."

"We have. I wanted to make real sure you were ready." The corners of Les' eyes crinkled up, so happy looking. "I sure am."

"Oh good." They started laughing together again, and it was good, so good, just holding each other.

Finally, though, Les turned, mouth meeting hers again, and the laughter faded away in favor of the heat that settled in her belly. His chest was rough with a light mat of hair, and his legs seemed to go on for miles.

One of his thighs slipped between hers, and she moaned, pressing back down against him.

"Oh, honey. You're wet for me." He murmured it against her neck, and it was unbearably intimate, what he said, and not a bit dirty.

"I want you, Les, so bad." She arched, hips rolling a little. "And you want me."

"I do." He licked her throat. "Honey, I got to ask. Are you...? Do we need to use rubbers?"

"No. No, I started... After you came down I went to the doctor's, because I knew we might end up here." Rose knew Les—she knew he wouldn't hurt her, wouldn't make her sick.

"Oh, thank God." He pushed a little, sliding between her legs, moving so his cock pressed against her lower belly.

"Uh-huh." She let her hand slide down, fingers circling the tip of Les' cock.

Wet, hot, it pushed between her fingers, Les' hips moving in a slow circle. "Oh. Oh, Rosie-girl. That's... Oh."

Yes. Yes, it was. He was…thick and long and so hot. She… Wow.

Les let her hold him for mere seconds. Then he was easing her hand away, giving her a wry laugh. "Make me go off like a rocket, you keep that up."

"Mmm." She got that. She felt like if he touched her slit, just once, she'd shatter, and she could go more than once. "I hear you, Les. I got you."

"You do, honey. You surely do." Kissing her mouth, Les moved into position, the head of his cock slipping between her legs. Ready.

She shivered and gasped a little, arching for him. Les moaned, licking her lower lip. Then he just went ahead and did the deed, spreading her wide and pushing inside her body.

"Les…" She stretched for him, eyes wide. *Oh. Oh, wow. That felt. Yeah.*

"Mmm. Yes, ma'am." Sweat beaded on his lip, on his throat. Les held still a moment, letting her adjust, shudders shaking his long form.

She leaned up, took a kiss, licking his lips for him. Les hummed, and suddenly they were moving, his chest brushing her breasts, his cock spreading her wide. The friction made her gasp. There wasn't an inch of him she didn't feel, not a minute where she didn't feel full and spread.

Les rocked, pushing in, pulling out. He started off with tiny movements, but got going faster, got moving with her. They found their rhythm, sure and steady, making the bedsprings creak, making her butt slide on the comforter.

One of his hands slid under her, the other touched her, starting with her hair, then her cheek. Les looked at her as if she was the most beautiful thing ever. Her entire body felt like it was on fire.

"Rosie." Skin so hot against hers, Les pushed and rocked, his chest hair making her nipples ache.

She got one hand on his chest, fingers sliding down the mat of blond curls as she touched his belly. Those heavy muscles rolled as he loved on her. He kissed like a man who knew what he was doing. Did other stuff like that too. There was no fumbling or hesitation or nothin'.

His fingers slipped down, touched her just so, and it was pure lightning, making her arch and cry out for him. She was so wet that he moved easily over her, right where they joined, then a little higher. His hips moved in counterpoint, hot as anything.

"Oh. Oh, Les. I… Please." She didn't know what she was asking for, just that Les could give it to her.

"Yeah. Oh, honey. Yeah." He plucked at the little bundle of nerves right there, his touch rough at the tips.

Her sounds were embarrassingly loud, wanton, but she couldn't hold them back. Les didn't seem to care. In fact, he urged her on, licking at her lower lip. Yeah, he was all over the noises. There was a spring of need, deep in her belly, and it twined tighter and tighter, leaving her shaking, bucking underneath him, taking him deep.

A deep groan tore from Les' chest. "Rosie. I can't hold it, girl."

"Uh-huh. Uh-huh." That was the best she could do, because she was toppling over the edge, pleasure crashing down over her.

There was a moment when it seemed like everything stopped, even their breathing. Then Les was grunting, filling her deep, his wetness so good in her, so right.

She wrapped her arms around his shoulders, fingers moving idly.

Les buried his face against her throat, breathing hard. He kissed the skin there, a damp little peck, and it made her smile.

"Will you stay the night, cowboy?" She couldn't stop touching him, loving on him.

"I will if you want me to, honey." Rolling to one side, just a little, Les slid one hand down over her hip, holding her close. "I would love that, in fact."

There was a spot for her head, right there on his shoulder. "I would too."

More than just about anything. All she had to do was smother those psycho voices in her head with a pillow.

Chapter Fourteen

Les woke up and was immediately aware of three things.

He was in a bed, which was an amazing luxury. The bed smelled like flowers and Rosie, not stale beer and Fritos. And the dog nibbling gently on his fingers was not a giant, slobbery wolfhound, which was what his buddy, Tug, was. This was a wee, wee Presley.

Man, life was good.

Bright black button eyes stared at him, that fluffy tail lifting and wagging.

"Hey, furball. How do you feel about bacon?" He'd cook up breakfast if Rosie had anything in the fridge.

The pup leaped into his arms, then licked his nose.

"I think that's a vote for lots of bacon. Come on, bud. Let's go potty, huh?" He figured the poor pup had to go.

He let the pup out onto Rosie's tiny patio, then headed to the kitchen.

Rosie's fridge had a huge plate of caramels, just for him, which gave him a happy, along with eggs, bacon, and a couple of packages of meat that he knew she'd bought to feed him. He munched a caramel while he pulled out the bacon and eggs. He didn't realize he was still in the buff until he turned the stove on and felt the heat.

Warm hands wrapped a robe around him, tucking his dangling bits behind the terrycloth. "Careful with you, now."

"Thanks, honey." Les turned around and kissed Rosie good morning, and he meant it. It was a good day already and high hopes for it getting better.

"Mmm. Coffee?" She wore a tiny tank top and little pink shorts and her hair... Oh, damn. He'd never gotten to see it, loose and down and so dark, hanging down past the curve of her backside.

"If you're making, I'll never turn it down." Les had to kiss her again. Had to. He bent to her lips, one hand cupping the back of her head behind her hair. So pretty. Lord, he could just wallow in her. Of course, then his pan started smoking and Presley started barking.

"Mmm. Bacon." She stepped back and her nipples were hard and Les thought he could smell that she wanted him as bad as he wanted her.

"Uh-huh." He could control himself until after breakfast. No, really. Even if his cock was trying to poke right out of the robe.

He turned the bacon, then headed for the fridge to get the eggs. That gave him a perfect view of...everything as Rosie bent to pull something out of the bottom drawer.

He almost crashed right into her when he stumbled. Damn. She was gonna be the death of him.

"Les?" She stood, glanced over her shoulder. "You okay, cowboy?"

"I am. I just... You're so pretty, honey." He smiled at her, patting her butt automatically.

"You make me happy. You hunting eggs?"

"I am. I'll be hunting you before it's over, though."
Might as well be honest.

Her pretty ass pushed right into his hand. "I should
hope so."

"Oh, good." That meant he could get through his
breakfast, knowing she was waiting too.

He managed the bacon, the eggs, without burning
anything, and Rose did toast and coffee and orange
juice. He sat down at the kitchen table, grabbing her as
she walked by. Her belly was soft where her wee top
inched up, and her breasts pressed against his cheek.
Lord, she was sweet.

Her curls tumbled around him as she leaned and
kissed the top of his head. "Hey."

Les breathed deep, humming a little. This was like
paradise to an old cowboy like him. Well, a not even
middle-aged one, really.

He slipped her right onto his lap, loving the soft
laugh, the way her breasts pressed against him.

"You're better than breakfast, Rosie." He patted her
butt, letting her wiggle on him.

She snatched up a piece of bacon, put it against his
lips. "You can have both."

"I can, huh? That's a fine thing." He munched his way
through the bacon, then the toast.

They managed their breakfast with her sitting right
there, snuggled in his lap like she belonged there.

She fed him bites and he slipped some between her
lips and man, it was weirdly hot. He'd always thought
it had to be chocolate syrup or something to be sexy
food. This was just breakfast, which they'd had several
times before. Just not after a night like last night.

When she leaned down and licked orange juice off his
bottom lip, Les gave that stupid line of had to be sexy

food thinking right on up. He pushed the plates away so they didn't break nothin', figuring it might be time to get a little busy.

"Am I too heavy? You're okay?"

He chuckled at her words. In some things, all girls were the same. She didn't weigh as much as a bird, his wee lady, but she worried.

"You're perfect." His hands shaped around her butt, those little shorts things not standing in his way at all. Lord, she was a wet dream.

"Mmm. Your hands are warm." She snuggled in and kissed him, her hands moving up to cup his face.

"Well, you're not exactly chilly, honey." No, sir. She was on fire.

She laughed against his lips, then turned to straddle his thighs, scoot forward until they were belly to belly.

"Oh. Hello." Hell yes, was what he really meant.

"Mmmhmm. Hey, cowboy." Snuggly girl. She unfastened the robe, then scooted in again. "This okay?"

It would be better if her little top was off.

"It's real good." He nuzzled right in, letting her feel how happy he was.

Those shorts were soft, teasing his most sensitive skin, and he reached for the bottom of her shirt. It was only fair.

He pulled it off over her head, her hair tickling him like crazy. Her breasts spilled out, pushing against his chest.

Her skin was pale, silky, and she smelled so good. Her nipples teased his skin, little points of heat.

Les reached up and touched one, plucking at it. Les loved the feel of her skin.

He loved those sweet, tiny noises she offered him too. Part moan, part needy cry — the sounds went straight to his cock. He rubbed up against her, separated from her by the tiniest strip of fabric. Lord. Please.

"I... I want..." She took his hand, slid it down between them. God, she was wet, slick.

"Me too." Oh, he so did. He wanted. He pushed his fingers under her panty-short things and rubbed them against the slickest skin ever, opening her up.

Rosie gasped, and her hips rocked, moving against his touch easy as anything.

"That's my girl." So wet for him. He lifted her with his other arm wrapped around her waist, pulling at the damned space-aged fabric.

She helped, swinging one leg around to get the damn things off, then straddling him again.

Fuck him raw. Les' eyes rolled back in his head, a rough moan coming from his chest. "Rosie. You ready to ride, girl?"

"I am."

His fingers were still working her, still loving on her, and she started to tremble.

"Me, too." Les reluctantly moved his hand, grabbing her hips to lift her up. "Get me in place?"

Her touch was hot where they wrapped around his shaft, hot enough that his hips bucked up.

He almost unseated them both with that smooth move, but he managed to hold it together. He guided her hips down, the head of his cock slipping inside.

Her lips parted, and he got another sweet little sound.

"Mmmhmm." Les kissed her open mouth, his tongue sliding right in just like his cock pushed inside her. She was damned perfect, made for him.

It didn't surprise him a bit, how they got their rhythm so easy. She fit perfect and they'd already danced.

Then she did this...thing with her muscles, and that did kind of surprise him. In the best possible way.

He stared at Rosie and she grinned, looking wicked as all get out. *Oh, sweet lady.*

Les let his hips go, let them rise and fall until the chair creaked, until shit on the table shook. He just went with it.

His hands wrapped around her butt, helping her move, and she pulled him into one kiss after another. His balls drew up hard, his cock swelling even more. God. He was just gonna explode.

He could feel her, the tight sheath around his shaft starting to ripple, to work him as she got close.

Les put in a superhuman effort to move his hand, and he pushed down, reaching for her clit. He needed her wild. Crazy.

"Les!" Oh.

Oh, sweet Jesus.

She arched back, her body bowed for him, letting him see everything as she bucked, rode him like a champ.

"Rosie." She was right there with him. They came within seconds of each other, both of them panting and shaking.

His girl. Good Lord, she was something.

Les stroked her back, up and down, then back up under her hair. He loved her hair.

"Mmm. Good morning, cowboy." So that was the sound of well-loved Rosie. Les approved.

"Morning, honey." Les rubbed noses with her. "That was a fine howdy."

"It was. It so was." She chuckled. "Thank you for breakfast."

"Not a problem. You let me sleep in a bed." That had been worth a little bacon splatter.

"You don't have a bed where you're staying?" A little line formed between her eyes.

"Huh?" Oh, shit. He didn't want her feeling sorry for him, now. "The screened-in porch smells better than sleeping inside."

"Les Jacoby! You… You need your rest. It's hot for you. You'll be all dehydrated!"

He blinked. "Well, I got a fan at the Wal-Mart."

"You…" She glared at him, stared him right down. "You can stay here. And I don't want to hear nothing about us making love and now I'm all moving you in and stuff. You can stay on the sofa if you don't want to share the bed, but that's not right, my cowboy, sleeping on a porch!"

Les blinked some more, then grinned. Then he might have whooped a little. "Your cowboy. Yes, ma'am. I am that."

"You are and I can't believe I never asked where you were staying." She took his face between her hands, kissed him but good. "You come stay here. I bet I smell way better than a bunch of cowboys."

"They have a big old dog, too." Well, that wasn't fair, really. So did Les, a dog who was probably missing him like crazy. "But I won't argue."

"Good man." Rose nodded. "This way you've got air conditioning."

"And a lovely roommate." He'd pay her rent. He'd been making enough with the riding.

"With a very tiny dog."

"Hey, at least everyone here bathes." He winked at her, not wanting to think on it too much more. "I'll get my stuff today."

"I'll go get you a key made." She grinned, hugged him a little. "I have to take the fuzzball to get groomed and get my hair cut."

"I can go food shopping if you want." He would pick up some guy snacks. "Just make me a list."

"We could go together, if you want, this afternoon…"

"Sure, honey. I can get my stuff, you can do hair, and we can meet back here." He grinned, loving the idea of doing something so simple and domestic with her.

"Sounds perfect." She kissed him. "After a shower. We smell like we've been naughty, you and me."

"I like it." He could see why she wouldn't want to go in public like that. "Come on, honey. We'll scrub."

She stood, and as he grabbed her ass, her laughter filled the little apartment up.

Chapter Fifteen

Rose grabbed the two bags from her baby truck and headed to the apartment. Les was riding down in Nagcodoches, but he'd be home for supper. Back for supper. Here. Whatever.

She knew he couldn't stay. She knew it. He had a life up in the mountains—a good job that he loved and friends and snow and stuff —but she liked to pretend it could last a little.

Once she'd given up on that whole 'not dating a cowboy' thing, anyway.

Hell, she'd been brave. She'd gone to see him ride in Canton. She'd cried through half the rodeo, but she'd gone. And watched. He hadn't smashed himself up or anything, but she'd still sat there with her heart half beating out of her chest. He'd taken one look at her face after and not asked her to come watch again.

She'd apologized about a million times, but he just kissed her, told her to hush.

Rose managed to get the door open and the groceries put down when her phone started ringing. Oh. Beau's name popped up. "Hey, Mr. Beau! How're you?"

"I'm good, Miss Rose. How are you?" He sounded pretty happy, which was always good.

"I'm good, sir. Real good. I'm fixin' to make enchiladas."

"Mmm. Wish I was comin' over." He chuckled. "Heard you were at the rodeo last weekend."

"Man, who told on me? I only saw one little roper kid I recognized, besides my Les."

Beau Lafitte knew the whole *world*.

"You remember that Brazilian boy that came to stay with Balta a few summers back? He's on the Texas circuit now. I think he had a crush on you."

"Nonsense!" She pinked right on up, though, pleased. "I went to see Les ride. He made the short go, made a check. I was proud." And scared half to death. Cheyenne?

"Good on him. Reckon I don't know this feller."

"He's from Colorado, not full-time rodeo. He works on a ranch." She started unpacking groceries. "Les Jacoby. You'd like him." Had she not mentioned Les in Cheyenne?

"I bet I would. You sure sound like you do."

She chuckled. "I do. I... You don't think it's wrong, do you? I mean, it's been a long time since..."

"No, ma'am. I think it's just fine." Beau paused a moment, and she could all but see what he called his thinking expression. "He just needs to be good enough for you, is all."

"He's a good man—he dances, Beau, and he likes Presley and he tuned up my truck." And he made love to her and made her feel like there wasn't anyone he'd rather touch.

"Well, I'm tickled. I am. He staying down your way?"

"He is. He's staying with me for a couple of weeks, till he has to go back to the mountains."

"Oh." She could hear the doubt start to creep in. "You going with him? We'd sure miss you."

"He hasn't asked. I... I don't know if he wants me, full-time yet. Hell, I don't have anything to offer, really. What would I do on a ranch? Stand around and take up space?" Oh. Oh, she hadn't thought all this out, had she? She could work cattle, but she knew nothing about a big operation.

"Oh, now, Rose. Don't go gettin' all upset on my account. I'm just a nosy old Cajun." Beau sounded as if he was talking to his granny.

"I just... Yeah. Yeah, I'm okay." Right?

"Well, then I'm happy. How's that job going?" Beau talked to her for near a half hour, telling her about the barn and the dogs and all sorts of things. By the time she'd started the hamburger, she was chuckling and promising to come out to Sammy's birthday party.

"Well, Miss Rose, I'll talk to you again in a few weeks, okay? I got an event to do announcing for down your way. Maybe we can have some supper."

"I'd love that, Beau. Honest. You just call." She hung up the phone and went to make tea.

It was maybe two hours later when Les came in, and she could smell him almost before she heard Presley go crazy. He'd brought Popeye's.

She chuckled, shook her head. Dear man. She did love him.

Rose stopped.

Blinked.

Christ on a crutch.

"Hey, honey." Les came walking over, long legs working, signs of arena dirt still on his jeans. "I got dinner about five minutes ago, so it ought to be hot."

"It smells so good." She lifted her face for a kiss. "There's enchilada stuff for later, too. How'd you do?"

Loved him.

She loved him.

"I did okay in the first round." He grinned a little, the expression crooked and rueful.

She patted his arm, gently just in case he was hurting. "You want a beer?"

"I would love one." He laid all the food out—chicken strips and potatoes, dirty rice and biscuits. And onion rings for her.

"Mmm. Onion rings." She grabbed two beers. "Beau said to say hi."

"Beau?" Les paused, a biscuit halfway to his mouth. "Lafitte? Is something wrong?"

"With who?"

"I don't know. I mean, someone like that called me, it would be to be the bearer of bad news." Les shrugged a little, cheeks pinking right up.

"Oh, no. Beau's my friend. He just checks in." She winked. "He heard I was seeing someone, I think, and he's a Cajun—he's nosy."

"Ah." Les grinned. "Well, he can rest easy. You're in good hands."

"I am." She handed him his beer. "Real good."

"C'mere." His fingers closed around her wrist, and he pulled her close with the hand not holding the beer. Les took a kiss that curled her toes and left her panting.

Oh.

Wow.

And also yum.

"Appetizer." He grinned, eyes sparkling. "Wait until you see what I do for dessert."

She laughed, reached up to cup his jaw. "Is there sugar involved?"

"There might just be." His lips grazed her fingers before Les moved away to fill a plate.

She stole an onion ring, crunching away. God, why couldn't they taste as good made at home?

"Did you want the biscuit, honey?" He was on biscuit three, and they'd given him four. Someone had worked up an appetite.

"No, love. I'm okay with the onion rings and chicken. Thank you."

Love.

She loved him.

So much for not dating a cowboy. Or falling for one. Now she was in love with one. And the smile he gave her was pretty fond in return, bright and happy. He even fed chicken to her dog.

She sat at the table, her mind going about a million miles a minute.

"A penny for them, honey." Those long fingers plucked up another onion ring so he could feed it to her.

"I..." She blinked, surprising herself by tearing up.

"What?" That panicky expression slid across Les' face. "What is it, Rosie?"

"I-I'm. I'm in love with you. I just... I've never been in love with anybody but Timmy before." Well, that was sophisticated and all...

The panic went away faster than it had come, and Les grabbed her, swinging her around. He might have whooped a little at her too. "You love me?"

"Uh-huh." She held on tight, those broad shoulders steadying her like it was nothing.

"Well, that's good, honey. I was worried." He kissed her, then. Hard. Happy.

That eased that hard little knot of worry in her chest, so she kissed him back, encouraging him to just make things easy. Better. He did. They left the food, as it was on the high counter and Presley couldn't do anything.

They left it because Les carried her right into the bedroom.

She wrapped her legs around his waist, and he sat, keeping her right there. His hands were under her butt, supporting her, and Les just kissed her like there was no tomorrow. Like all he ever had to do in life was kiss her. Rose felt as if she was floating, flying. His eyes were open, watching her, and it made her shiver. Those blue eyes were just... They shone for her, full of emotion. She could almost hope.

She moaned when the kisses got slower, softer, making her dizzy.

Les started on her clothes, on her top, pulling it off. His hands were so gentle on her. Every touch made her shake a little, made her push closer.

"Look at you." He stroked the top of her breast, right above the line of her bra. "So pretty."

"Yeah? You think so?"

"No, Rosie. I *know*. You're beautiful, and you're all mine." He kissed her again, his hands sliding up her back. Oh God. She was. She so was.

Rose arched back into Les' hands, crying out as their bellies rubbed.

Les bent to her throat, licking, biting a little. He never bruised or anything, but he let her know how much he wanted her. Then Les' mouth moved to her breast, lips wrapping around her nipple. He sucked, pulling strongly at her, making her moan and twist, the pleasure like lightning as it zipped through her body. It was as if he knew her already, knew what would make her crazy.

That pressure and pull felt like there was a string attaching her nipple and her center, the tug amazing.

Les moaned for her, lips opening a moment so he could mutter something, then closing on her other nipple. Focused.

Rose couldn't help moving, her entire body shifting against Les' thighs. His body rocked against her in return, his muscles like steel bands under her legs and hands. When she pushed his shirt off, she could see a smattering of bruises from his rides, right there on his chest.

"Baby..." She leaned in, kissed each bruise gently.

"What?" Peering down at himself, Les chuckled. "It wasn't all that bad."

"Still. Poor cowboy." She kissed the bruises again. "You smell good."

"Yeah?" His fingers worked through her hair, freeing it. "I love your hair, honey."

She flushed dark, let her head fall back.

"It's so heavy, so good in my hands."

Her whole body flushed as his fingers dragged through her hair, petting her. Nuzzling in under the side of the heavy fall, Les licked along her neck, his fingers finding her nipples. He never stayed in one place too long, just explored all of her.

Soon she was arching, crying out for him, begging for him. "Les..."

Les nodded, panting a little. "Need you, honey. Can I... We still got these pesky bottoms."

"Uh-huh." She stood up, stripping off her jeans like the worst kind of slut.

Les struggled out of his so fast she figured he'd leave skid marks. Then he was pulling her back down. She straddled him, leaned in to bring their lips together. Her cowboy.

She was just as much his too. She loved the way he felt against her, the way his chest hair rubbed her and made her more than a wee bit crazy. His hands slipped down her sides, fingers wrapping around her hips.

"My girl." He grinned at her before rolling up a little to nibble at her neck.

"Mmmhmm. That feels so good, cowboy."

"You taste good." They were basking in each other, but that was okay.

She chuckled, brushing through Les' hair. So thick, heavy, and a little bit slick. It clung to her fingers right next to his skull, slid away when she got out toward the ends. It was kind of fascinating. She moaned softly, rocking on his lap. "I could touch you forever."

"Well, I ain't gonna argue with that."

"No? Might scare some guys away."

"Not this one." His hands moved over her, sure and confident. Never faltering.

"Good." She took herself another kiss, her body sliding up along the hard shaft.

"Uh-huh. Real good." That man could sound plumb dirty when he wanted to.

She leaned back, fingers wrapping around his hardness so she could rub the tip against that tiny bundle of nerves that felt so good.

"Oh, honey." He shuddered, and his skin rose up with goosebumps.

"Uh-huh." Her eyelids were heavy, need pulsing in the pit of her belly.

"I can't wait no more, Rosie." Les moved her into position, shifting her so he could push inside. She took him all in, moaning long and low as he stretched her wide. Les moaned, too, his forehead resting against hers. God, he was hot and fine.

"Cowboy." She clenched her thighs and started moving, riding up and down, everything inside her singing. Les' singing was a little more tangible. He did like to make noise. Her strong, silent cowboy. She tightened as she pulled up, his shaft dragging inside her. That made him grunt, made him grab at her hips. Those hands clamped down on her skin, Les yanking her down, then helping her back up. Down. Up. Things got a little wild then, her sounds more and more embarrassing, louder and louder.

They were together in it, though. Les slapped against her, a little crazy, getting a little clumsy.

"Les!" One of his hands slid around, touched her right where she needed it.

"Yeah, honey. So wet for me." He moved his fingers in time with his hips.

She nodded. For him. Just for him. Her body tightened, her toes curled. Just as if she was an overwound spring, she snapped when Les hit that spot inside her, his fingers pressing her hard at the same time.

Rose heard him cry out, distantly, the moan almost like she'd done it herself. Les' eyes went wide and hot, and the man bucked like a bronc, and he filled her deep, wet and good.

His arms held her close, fingers sliding down her back in long strokes.

"My girl." He sounded so proud. Happy. She'd done that.

"My cowboy." She sighed and cuddled, leaning hard.

"You know it, Rosie. Balls to bones."

She thought she could live with that.

Chapter Sixteen

Rose pulled into the parking lot of the Roy H. Laird Memorial Hospital, sliding into a visitor spot near the doors of the emergency room.

Les had called half an hour ago, saying he was heading in, he'd gotten stepped on. Don't worry. No big deal. Right.

No big deal, except that Les was in the emergency room.

She ran inside, headed right up to the big window. "I'm here for Les Jacoby."

"Sure, honey. He's right back in exam three." Well, the admission lady didn't seem worried, so that was a good sign.

"Thank you, ma'am. Buzz me in?" She smiled at the girl, nodding as the door opened. Three. God, she hated hospitals. "Les?"

"Rosie?" She heard his voice, a little rough, but talking. To her. Knowing her name.

"Yes." *No crying. None. Zero.* "I got here as fast as I could."

"Well, hey. Honey." Les smiled at her when she got where she could see. The gash on his arm was almost all stitched up already.

"What happened?" No puking. No crying. No hysterics.

The little doctor man just chuckled but kept working without saying anything.

Les shook his head. "Well, I didn't get out of the way fast enough, did I?"

She winced, took a step closer. "A horse get you?"

"Uh-huh. Pick up man."

"Ouch. Do you... Do you need anything right now?"

"I could use a water, honey." He smiled gently at her, calm as still water.

"Okay. I'll grab a bottle." She nodded, heading out of the bay, down the hall. She made it to the bathroom before the tears came, the sobs hitting her so hard they scared her a little. She couldn't do this. She couldn't. The last time she was in a hospital she'd been with Timmy. Timmy's body because he'd been dead before he even left the arena. Broken.

Gone.

"Oh, God. Please..." She'd loved Timmy, so much, and she loved Les now, and she just... She couldn't do this.

She let herself cry it out, cry until she didn't have anything left, then she washed her face with the coldest water she could stand.

Okay.
Okay.
Mascara. Powder. Water for Les.
Coping.
Coping.

She'd decided to love her a cowboy again—a rodeo cowboy—she could damned well cope. She wasn't a baby.

When she got back to the bay, the doctor man was gone, and Les was resting back on the gurney, which was set up like an adjustable bed.

"Water. How long do you have to stay before I take you home?"

"Huh?" He looked a little woozy, one eye drooping a bit. "Oh. They want me to stay and get a shot or something."

"'Kay." She opened the bottle and handed it to him, then perched on the uncomfortable plastic chair.

"Thanks, honey." His gaze sharpened a little. "You okay, Rosie girl?"

"I'm not the one to worry about, Les." No. No, she wasn't okay, but she wasn't a giant dingbat, either. Now that the storm had passed, she could soldier on.

"Oh, I'm all right." He chuckled, sounding gravelly. "I swear, honey, I was sitting on my butt watching the bull riding."

"Damn bull riders." She winked, tried to keep it together.

"Shit. It was the bull. He crashed the gate, knocked three of us off the fence. The pick-up man ran me over when I bounced."

"Who was it? Gerardo Pena or Jim Hostler's boy?" Gerardo's wife, Mariposa, made the best tamales, ever.

"Hostler." Les laughed out loud. "You do know your stuff."

"I used to be married to a bull rider. I know how it works. You learn quick to know all about rodeo because it's the most important thing." Those men were cowboys first, husbands second.

"Yeah." Les sobered a little. "I'm just fine, honey."

"I'm glad." She dug around in her purse for some Tylenol. "What do you want for supper?"

"Something that's not crunchy." He laughed a little. "Maybe breakfast food?"

"Waffles and bacon it is." She found the little bottle, took two. "How're you doing?"

"Well, it hasn't started to throb again, yet." Les held out a hand to her. "Come sit here?"

"You sure?" At his nod, she slid over, fingers twining with his.

No crying.

None.

Zero.

"Uh-huh." He pulled her close. "Oh, honey, I'm sorry. I didn't mean to upset you."

"You didn't." She leaned in hard. "I'll get better at this. I promise." After all, she loved him.

"I hope you won't have to." He kissed the top of her head. "I'm not much of a rodeo man, really."

"I know that gets in your blood. I know." She did. She'd loved a bull rider. They were the worst.

"I do it to make money." That chuckle vibrated against her arm. "I can't complain. It got me you."

"It did." She was his. All of her.

"Well, we just need to get me that shot of germ killers and we can get on out of here." Les' nose twitched, and she knew it was all that antiseptic smell getting to him.

She nodded, kissed his chin. "We'll take my truck home and then I'll get somebody to drive me out here after you're settled to pick yours up."

"Oh, I can get one of the boys to bring me out tomorrow, honey."

The doctor man saved her an argument, coming in with a sterile tray. "This will be just a load of antibiotics. Your tetanus is up to date, thankfully."

"Is the muscle okay? It's just skin?"

"There's not going to be any permanent damage." The doctor smiled and patted her shoulder before going to do the hand sanitizer and glove thing. "It will be sore, certainly. There's some tissue swelling. He'll need to elevate."

"I can do that. Are you sending him home with pain meds?"

"I can write a prescription if you like. Over-the-counter NSAIDS will be a great help, too."

"Just tell me what you want me to do, and I'll take care of him."

He was hers, after all.

"I'll give you a list." Quick as a bunny, the doc did his thing, which was real nice, she figured, because usually they made a tech do all that.

Les didn't fuss any, which didn't surprise her. Hell, the money was the worst part. Damn little shows didn't have a sports medicine team.

* * * *

They finally got on the road, Les folded into her truck without too much trouble. Bless his heart.

"Do you want me to take you straight home and then fill your prescription?"

"Oh, honey, you don't have to do that tonight, you don't want to." Les was already nodding a little, eyelids so heavy.

"Hush." She'd just stop on the way home and he could nap in the truck. Maybe she'd buy herself a little bitty bottle of rum and a Coke, just to take the edge off.

"Okay. I can wait in the truck." He patted her hand, a little clumsy.

"Okay, sweetheart." She pulled into the Brookshires, picking up a few groceries, bandages, Neosporin, and a cheap bottle of wine while she waited on the pharmacy.

The lady at the pharmacy counter wanted to ask, she could tell. Thank God she didn't, or Rosie might have burst into tears. She got her bill paid, got the stuff to her baby truck, smiling at the sight of Les sleeping in the passenger seat.

She was so screwed.

So utterly screwed.

* * * *

Lord, Les was sore. Itching. Tired.

And feeling like a heel because he'd snapped at little Presley for stepping on his arm. What kind of idiot yelled at a dog just because he was aching?

Rose had hopped right up, given him pills and a Coke, then taken Presley for a walk, promising to bring home some burgers. She was a queen among women, but Les hated that she was walking on eggshells around him. He really did.

It didn't make sense and it made a load of sense, all at the same time. Cowboys got hurt—rodeo or not. Fencing, roping, riding, critters, there wasn't a bit of the work that couldn't get a man injured. Still, he figured getting hurt in the rodeo made Rosie more sensitive to his mood, more jumpy. That didn't seem right, but he sure didn't know how to stay near her without riding to make the money.

He got up, started pacing, trying to not feel like there just wasn't enough room to stretch out in Rosie's baby apartment. It was just his mood, not something real. Les wasn't one to dwell on shit—the day was too short usually. Rosie was worth some thought, though. Worth giving up the show, one hundred percent.

Maybe he could make some side money working construction instead. Or building fences. There was enough of that work in Longview that he could stop being lazy and trying to make easy money riding.

Once he got home—got her home, really, because that's what he wanted, wasn't it? His girl, home with him at the ranch—then he'd be okay. The boss was a solid man and that family had owned the land for generations. Les' daddy had been the foreman there until he'd passed and he figured, eventually, that'd be his spot too.

Not that he wanted anything to happen to the gent holding the job now. Montgomery was a good man. Solid as the day was long.

One way or the other, he wanted to take Rosie home and show her his mountains, play with her in the snow, take her out riding in the springtime. His girl would wear pink ropers, he'd bet, and they'd get her a small mare, surefooted and calm.

The door opened and in came his girl, carrying a bag of burgers, Presley trailing along, nose in the air, sniffing. Les didn't blame the little feller. The bag of burgers smelled good.

"I brought greasy lunch and walked him hard so he'd sleep."

"I sure am sorry I snapped." He smiled at her, hoping to help ease things, let her know he'd had an attitude adjustment. "But thank you."

"You're hurting. I get that." She grinned at him, warm as could be. "You got something to drink still? I couldn't juggle dog and food and cups."

"I do. You want a Coke?" He wasn't laid up or anything. He could walk to the fridge.

"Please, thank you." She offered him a smile that warmed him down to his toes.

"You got it." Rosie liked those red drinks, so he grabbed one for her and a bottle of water for him.

The burgers and fries were spread out all fancy on the table, the sight making him grin.

"What?" she asked and he shrugged.

"I like how you make the world a prettier place, Rosie." Les liked all the little touches, the way she wanted things to be nice for him. It made him want to do for her, as well.

"Enough of the world is harsh, huh? This should be good."

"You're amazing, sweet lady." He brought over the drinks, stopping to kiss the top of her head.

"Well, you're my cowboy and I intend to keep you happy, so…" She lifted her face and he kissed her lips.

He intended to keep her too—he just had to figure out how to do it without screwing up everything.

Chapter Seventeen

Rose did her best to not cry when Les headed off each weekend. It wouldn't do any good. It hadn't with Tim—that was for sure.

Rodeo people were rodeo people—the good and the bad parts—and she either had to live with it or leave and she couldn't make Les leave. She didn't want to.

She tidied up the apartment, then sat down at her little desk to maybe write a letter or two. She had to send a birthday card to Timmy's daddy, and— Oh, who was she kidding? She needed to get out for a bit.

She grabbed her phone and dialed Lindsay, hoping that she wasn't in the middle of huge plans with her husband, Frankie.

"Hello?"

"Linds? It's me. You busy?"

"Busy sitting on my fat ass. Matt's golfing. You?"

"Going stir crazy. Wanna go shop flip-flop clearance or something?" Old Navy always had a good deal or two.

"God yes. Please? Come get me?"

Twenty minutes later she had a very pregnant best friend in her truck and they were heading into town. They sang along with Miranda Lambert, the air cranked up so Lindsay didn't get nauseated.

"So, how's things with tall, blond and cowboy-y?" Lindsay asked.

Rose cackled and shook her head. "That was bad."

"He is, though. Come on. Tell." Lindsay poked her ribs.

"Les is… Well, he's amazing. I'm trying so hard to be a good girlfriend, you know? Understanding about the rodeo and all?" It was hard, though, because, while she understood just fine, she still didn't love it. She loved Les.

"Have you told him about Timmy?" Linds scowled. "Why do you have to be understanding? Why can't he?"

"Because he's working. I don't know. He's not like Timmy." Timmy had been in love with the idea of cowboys. He'd thought the rodeo was all about romance and what you saw in the movies.

Les, he was so practical. Darned humble. And he was riding the circuit in Texas to stay close to her. How could she bitch?

"Well, I still think you should tell him it bothers you."

"He knows, I think. I sort of almost passed out at the one event I came to."

Lindsay looked at her askance. "You did not!"

"Almost. I did go to the bathroom and puke. That's so gross. You hate for people to hear that in the stalls next to you."

"Tell me about it." Lindsay patted her pregnant belly.

Rosie grimaced. "You win. I swear, you tossed your cookies every hour for three weeks back at the beginning."

"Yes. God. Oh, you want to go get tacos after we shop? I love tacos."

"You hate spicy food," Rosie teased.

"Yes, but the baby loves it! Just like its daddy."

"Where do you want to go? Taco Bueno? Jucy's?" Rosie could murder a cheesecake chimichanga, but Jucy's had cinnamon bites.

"Yes. Either. Both. I'm easy." Linds grinned over. "First though, flip-flops and you have to try on cute clothes so I can be envious of your tiny heinie."

"We need to get you more stretch mark cream, too." Lindsay's husband apparently loved to rub in the creamy, soothing stuff.

Linds got a wickedly naughty grin on her face. "Yep. I'm telling you, honey. The best part about being this pregnant is the sex."

"The sex is pretty good without it." Oh, it had been so long since she could tease about that without feeling like a liar.

"Uh-huh. This is like magic."

"You're lying!" She had given up on babies with Timmy. Could she let herself imagine that with Les?

"Not even."

Her cheeks heated. "Well, maybe someday I'll get to try it." She could definitely see that. Babies with Les. Little blond cowboys and brunette girls wearing pink.

Oh, please, she prayed. *If You will it. I'd be a good momma and I'd love him forever, rodeo or not.*

"You will, honey." Lindsay sounded so firm, so sure. "You were born to be a mom. And you're what? Four years younger than me? You have tons of time."

"Thanks, Linds." She hugged her best friend, cracking up when the baby tried to karate kick her. "Oh, wow. So strong!"

"Right. Special teams, baby. Kicker."

She touched the hard belly, shook her head. "My godbaby. I'm so excited to meet him."

"Either way they'll play football."

She laughed. "With Matt as a daddy? Absolutely."

"I'm so glad you called today. I was fixin' to be all miserable." Lindsay wiped her eyes, but Rosie didn't mention it. She just handed over a Kleenex.

"Me too." She hooked her arm in Lindsay's after her friend wiped. "Let's go play, girlfriend."

She'd stress Les' rodeoing later. When she was alone.

* * * *

Les was about fifteen minutes out of Longview when his phone rang. He hit the button on his dash, keying up his fancy hands-free gadget, a gift from his sister last year.

"Hey, Lester."

Speak of the devil. "Hey, Hes. What's up?"

"I'm getting a pedicure. How'd you ride?" She loved to get an update, and pedicures made her feel guilty for sitting and doing nothing.

"I did all right." He's doubled his entry fee and gas, but that wasn't gonna pay a lot of bills.

"That sounds cheery. How's that pretty little girl you're so taken with?"

"She's amazing." A little freaked out. Beautiful.

"So, when are you going to snatch her up?"

"Soon, I hope." Hell, he didn't know what to do. He worked a dangerous job even at home. "She needs time to get used to me cowboying."

"Cowboying or rodeoing?" Hes' voice was sharp as a tack.

"Rodeoing. Her husband died riding bulls, Hester Ann."

He swore to God he could hear her eyes roll. "I'm fully aware of that, you asshole. You think I wouldn't research the girl that took you away from the ranch?"

"How?" He sounded like a rube. You could find anything on the Internet these days.

"Google. Duh. The video of her husband is everywhere. That's awful. I can't imagine that. Like Lane Frost."

Lord. He'd never looked it up. "Thing is I can't figure out how else to stay here with her."

"So, take her up with you. I mean, you can't stay down there. It's hot and we need you home."

"I want to, but she's a bayou girl." Was that a lame excuse? Maybe he was just afraid she'd say no.

"What are you going to do, brother?"

"I'm gonna see if the boss will take me back now instead of the end of the summer. If I give up the show, she might come with me, right?" He wanted to be with Rosie so much more than he wanted anything else. Time to frickin' commit.

"You know he will, and if she needs you to give it up, then...fuck her. She should be willing to risk it, just like you should be willing to give it up."

"She's brave as hell, Hes. I know it. I just hate asking her to give up her whole life." Although maybe he needed to let her make the decision. Shit, he didn't know.

"You should talk to her, huh? Let her know what's important." Hes was even more practical than he was.

Yeah, talking wasn't always his strong suit, but darn it, Rosie needed to hear some things. "I will. I promise."

"Good man. Go. Make with the whole girlfriend thing so you can come home. I miss you."

"We'll have Italian."

"Cheap Italian, even. They opened a Beau Jo's, Lester."

"Oh, damn and also, hell yes. I'll be there soon." Beau Jo's. Mile High pizza. With honey for the crust. Uhn. He'd been to the original place in Idaho Springs many times.

"You'd better be." Hes laughed. "Tell her. She sounds like she's worth it."

He nodded. She was. Rosie totally was his girl.

Chapter Eighteen

Rose had the fried chicken done about the time she saw Les pull into the parking lot from the kitchen window.

She always wondered how the ladies in the fifties fried chicken in pearls and frilly aprons and perfectly coiffed hair. Every time she cooked it, she ended up looking like a grease stain had given her a hug.

She ran into the bedroom to change into a pair of shorts and a clean tank top, managing to scrub her face and pin her hair up in a mess before her cowboy made the stairs.

Did she have time for lip gloss? She grabbed a tube of ChapStick so she could look...what? Kissable? *Hi, I smell like batter and grease. Kiss me.*

She started giggling, and by the time Les walked in, she was laughing hard, holding her stomach.

"Rosie? Hey, puppers, where's your momma?" Les found her a few moments later, Pres trailing behind. "Hey, honey. You okay?"

"I am. I'm a mess, but there's homemade fried chicken."

"Smells real good." Les seemed fine, no new bruises to be seen. His back would be all covered in them because bareback riding did that, but he didn't seem to be moving too careful. Thank God.

"It is. I stole a nibble." She headed over for a kiss. "I boiled potatoes, but I didn't know if you'd want mashed or potato salad."

"Whatever is easiest for you, sweet lady." Les bent easily, taking her offered lips with a low hum of happy pleasure.

Oh, he tasted like mint and happy man. She did love that, and Rosie clung to his upper arms, her body ready even if her brain said she needed to do something with those potatoes.

"Mmm. Love coming home to those kisses, Rosie."

He straightened up, back popping. Poor baby. "Do you need some Tylenol, cowboy?"

"Nope, I'm solid. Been doing some thinking, that's it. That's tough for my type."

She swatted his arm. "Dork."

"Well, now, you know it's true." Those blue eyes twinkled. "Feed me and I'll tell you all about it."

"Let me throw the green beans on and I'll mash the potatoes. Do you need gravy?"

"Not unless you want to make it. Yum." His expression said *oh, gravy, please.*

"I can make some up. Have a sit and I'll stir while you share your thoughts." She wanted to know what had gotten him so thoughtful.

"Thanks, honey." He grabbed a Coke out of the fridge. He moved easier in his skin today, as if he'd taken a weight off his mind.

She poured out the grease from the frying pan and heated it up, then grabbed the corn starch and the shaker bottle.

"So you don't use a roux?"

"Listen to you!" She loved when Les knew something she didn't expect him to. "I figured cream gravy would just be too heavy for this hot of a day."

"Chicken gravy, then. I do love homemade gravy." Les made a show of lip smacking.

"Well, thank goodness I've made lots, then." Boys and their gravy. Rosie liked a little on her potatoes, but heaven knew Timmy had smothered his food in the stuff.

"Yep." Les sat back watched her, a smile crinkling up his laugh lines.

"So, what's on your mind, cowboy?" Salt, pepper, stir stir stir. She watched the wooden spoon scrape up all the good bits.

"Well, I got to thinking on this trip. I think for the rest of the time I'm down here I'll do some day labor. Construction or something. No more rodeoin'."

"What? Why?" She didn't understand. Didn't Les come here for the longer circuit? Because Texas was rodeo central and he could make money?

"Well, honey, it upsets you so." He seemed so pleased with himself.

"But... You don't have to give it up. I've been trying hard not to be a freak."

"You haven't been." Les spread his hands, his riding hand sporting blue and purple bruises. "I just know it worries you and you're special to me."

She kept stirring, staring down into the gravy. "And I know it's important to y'all cowboys. It's like a drug or something. I wouldn't ask you to change, Les. It wouldn't be love if I did that."

"Oh, Rosie, it's just a job. I make more money at it than I do at the ranch, you know?" He looked so...pleased with himself.

Her hand tightened around the handle of the spoon and it shook a little. "Just a job?"

"Well, yeah." The chair scraped on the floor when he stood to move up behind her. "It's just something I'm okay at."

"Then why do you do it? I mean, why would you?" Tears began to slide down her cheeks, hot and bitter. "Why would anyone do it?"

"Well—I mean, I grew up with it, honey." He put his hands on her shoulders, long fingers warm.

"He died because it was the most important thing in the world. He died on the dirt because getting out there and winning was better than life. I could understand that. Loving something so much you couldn't say no." She'd loved Timmy that much and she was pretty afraid she loved Les that much too.

"Now I've hurt your feelings." Les squeezed her shoulders. "I wasn't trying to."

"No. No, I'm not hurt, I'm angry. If you don't love it, then it's not worth it. You get hurt, Les. You get hurt for money. It's not like you were doing something good, something honest and real and right! This is a fucking game and people die!" She clapped her hand over her mouth, shocked at herself. "Oh, God. I'm sorry."

"No." He reached past her and turned off the stove. Then Les spun her around and stared into her eyes. "No, you don't be sorry. You lost someone you loved."

"I did. I loved him so much and now... God, I love you. I never thought I'd ever love another guy, much less a cowboy, and I'm trying so hard to be brave." But she wasn't. She was a damn coward—scared of losing Les, scared of living this crappy little life where she was just a...a... Just somebody who used to be married to a good guy.

"I love you, too, honey. That's what I'll give up the game. You mean so much more to me than ropes and broncs."

"I..." She pushed into his arms, crying hard. She didn't want him to think badly on her, but... She'd loved Timmy too.

"Shh. I got you, honey." He wrapped his arms around her. "I'm sorry."

"I don't want to burn your gravy." They leaned together like little children, trapped in a hurricane. "I promised myself I wouldn't love a cowboy again."

"Well, I reckon I'm glad you changed your mind." He kept pressing kisses to her hair.

"I hope so. It would suck if you didn't care." She met his eyes, knowing she looked a mess. "Because I'd be with you, even with the rodeo."

"I know you would, and that means the world to me." Les stroked her hair. "You know, when I go back to ranch work, that's not a cakewalk."

"I grew up on a rice farm, Les. I know from hard work. I'm not going to burst into tears from having to pay bills or anything. I just... I want to work *for* something."

"I want you." Les kissed the tip of her nose.

God, she hoped so. She hoped he would ask—well, that was a thought for another time.

For right now she just wanted this to be real.

More than that, she *needed* it to be real.

Chapter Nineteen

Les' cell rang about seven a.m., waking him from a real nice dream. Then he felt Rosie pressed against him and realized it wasn't a dream. No, sir, it was real.

He slid out of bed, goosebumps rising on his skin from the AC. He grabbed his phone and Presley, tossing the wiggling bundle of white fur out to go to the bathroom.

"Hello?"

"Hey, Les." *Oh. Harris. The boss.*

"Hey, boss. How's it going up there?" Les checked the flowery little calendar on the wall. Oh, good. He wasn't supposed to check in for a few days yet.

"Good, busy. How's the riding?"

"Well, it was going good until I decided to stop. My last ride was bumpy." He rolled his eyes at his forearm, the stitches black and gross, then glanced over his shoulder. "The girl is going better."

"Yeah? You bringing her home, son? We could fix up that one frame house."

"I hope so, sir." He was gonna ask finally. See what she said. "One way or the other, I'll be up there to move the herd."

"Glad to hear to. We lost Montgomery. His momma's got the cancer. He ain't coming back, so I'll need you to take charge." Montgomery had been Mr. Harris' foreman for…years. Since Les' daddy had passed on.

"Oh, damn. You got an address for him, I'll send a note." Surely Rosie had some of them cute cards that said sympathy shit.

"Yeah. Yeah, I do. You… You reckon you're interested in the foreman slot? It'd mean a year-round gig."

"I'd love to, boss, but I can't guarantee it. If Rosie is set on staying in Texas, well, I'll have to come back to her." The words surprised him when they came out. He'd never even thought about staying in Texas full-time.

"Well, I'll give you a bit to work that out, 'fore I find someone else." The boss grunted. "You're the one I want for the job. Always knew when Montgomery went I would ask."

"Thank you, Jim." That made him proud, made his chest swell up. "I'd be tickled."

"Good. You tell that gal we'd be pleased to have her, if she should come."

"I will. Thank you. I'll call in a week and a half or so, let you know when to expect me."

"Sounds good. Take care. Good ride."

"See you soon." Les hung up, feeling like he was on a big old teeter-totter. Up and down, worse than riding any bronc. Change was tough for a stubborn guy like him.

"Cowboy?" Soft hands slid up his back. "You okay?"

"Hmm? Morning, Rosie." He let her lean on him, warming up his skin. "I'm good. How are you?"

"Happy. You want some coffee?" Her hands slid around his belly, loving on him.

"I do." He put his hands over hers, swaying gently.

"That your boss on the phone?"

"It was. He—" Shit, they hadn't been together any time, really, but he couldn't hide anything from her. "He wants me to run foreman."

"Oh, yeah? Good for you!" She kissed his shoulder, squeezed him. "Do you have to leave early?"

"Not for another week or so." He didn't want to ask her yet. He wanted to feel her out on snow and mountains and how different Colorado was from Texas or Louisiana. He knew she loved him, but what did that mean for the rest of their lives?

"Oh, good." She took a shaky little breath, held on.

"Mmm." Les let her for a moment, but then he pushed away enough to turn so he could kiss her. She lifted her face to him, easy as pie. Les kissed her, trying to be gentle, but he was a little nervous, a little afraid. So he was a bit clumsy.

Rosie chuckled, hands framing his face. "It's okay, cowboy. I know you can't stay here forever."

"I-I want to be with you, honey. One way or the other."

"I know." Her eyes were shining, staring up at him. "I'm gonna miss you, so bad."

"You could come with me." Okay, so much for not asking now. He just blurted it out.

"Is there a place for me there? Work for me to do?"

"The boss says he would redo the old foreman's house. Been empty a bit, because Montgomery stayed in the bunkhouse. Might take until spring to get it fixed up." His heart started to pound. "Work, well, I reckon we'd find something for you to do for work. Hell, Harris would pay you to make pralines and caramels."

"Well, we should talk about it then. Plan. If we have until spring I'll start gussying up my resume and seeing what I need to do to move." That was his dear, practical girl. So ready to tie her wagon to his, but wanting to do something.

"We should." He would come back here if she wouldn't go north. In the spring after he'd fulfilled his duty to Harris.

"We'll figure something out. Assuming some pretty Colorado cowgirl doesn't steal your heart away in the meantime."

"Well, they had years to steal me, and it took you to do it." He grinned down at her.

"I was busy being sad and stuff. Mourning." She leaned a little. "Timmy wouldn't've liked you. He would have been jealous. I think...I think he'd understand, though. That I fell in love."

"You think so?" He hoped so. He sure hoped a cowboy like that would want his lady to be happy.

"I do." Her chuckle was soft. "Not that I fall for cowboys, you know."

"Nope. Not a bit." He laughed, feeling lighter now.

"There's my smile." She kissed his nose. "Now I'll make coffee."

"Okay, honey." He patted her butt. Man, how had he missed those teeny shorts?

More importantly, how had he missed taking advantage of it? His hands clenched a little. Her hips swayed, side to side, perfect as could be. Les watched, his head moving in time. "Uh. You want me to start bacon?"

"Sure." She bent over to scratch Presley. *Wow. Curvy. Amazing.*

He reached right out, shaping to her derriere. *Hoo.*

"Mmm. That's not bacon." She chuckled, went up on tiptoe.

"Nope. It's more like rump roast." She was gonna whack him so hard.

"Oh, I am gonna kick your butt." She stood up, turned and popped him in the arm, which got him full-on boobies.

Little cotton tank top. Bouncing. He drooled.

"Are you laughing at me?" She hit him again, and that made everything bounce.

"No, ma'am. I am not. I am staring at your boobs."

"Les!" Rosie giggled, tugged down the top of her tank, her nipples just peeking.

"Mmmhmm." He grabbed those, too, pushing his hands up under her breasts to help those nipples pop up.

Oh, look at those...

He bent and kissed one, lips brushing the tip. Pretty, pretty girl.

His pretty girl.

Rosie's nipple perked right up, just begging for attention. God, she was responsive. And she wasn't shy. Her hands found the back of his neck, holding him there while he sucked.

"Oh..."

He could listen to that happy, horny little sound for the rest of his life.

Hell, he would, except he was making some pretty good noises of his own.

She leaned back against the counter, arching up into his mouth.

He might just fall over. *Damn. Damn.* He was shaking, hands on her, trying to get her closer. He slid his hands down her thighs, spreading them, fingertips stroking her curls. The shorts just slid away to give him access, and Les bent to lick at her thigh, needing to taste. She smelled so good—citrusy and womanly and fine. He nibbled some, just humming, his tongue pushing against her. God, yeah.

"L-Les." Her voice sounded so husky, so harsh.

"Mmm." He found her center, closing his lips around her tiny nerve bundle. That earned him the best cry, Rosie calling to him, the sexiest thing he'd ever heard. Such an amazing thing, this part of a woman. So sensitive. She trembled for him, her folds swelling at the touch of his tongue. He could taste it, when she was ready for him. Feel it against his mouth. He stood straight.

"Please. I need." She panted, stared at him.

"I know. I know, honey." Thanking God one more time that she was a smart lady, he pushed against her, his cock spreading her. She took him in, wet and soft and hot and so fine. Les thought he might be ready to die a happy man. He moved his hips in a tiny circle, his breath catching.

"Yes." Fuck, she was pretty.

"Rosie." How was he gonna leave her if she didn't come with him?

She nodded, moaned for him, body tight around him.

"My girl." That was all there was to it. His. He'd figure out what he needed to do to keep her.

"Yes." Rosie bucked, nails digging into his upper arms. "Need. Please, Les."

"Okay, honey. I got you." It wasn't like he'd forgotten what he was doing. He'd just gotten wrapped up in his feelings and stopped moving. Now he remembered how. He was a cowboy, after all.

Those pretty, pretty eyes went wide-wide, and Rosie cried out, grunting and grinding against him.

"Come on, sweet girl. Come on." His balls were aching, begging him to let the pressure loose.

He got a single, quick nod, and she whimpered, wet and shaking as she came for him.

"God, girl. You rock my world." His voice was shaking as hard as all his muscles.

Her body squeezed him, her lips parted and wet. "Mmm. Your turn, cowboy."

"My-my turn." He grunted, shaking, moving fast for maybe three seconds before he lost it.

Her lips brushed over his face, loving on him as he shook through his orgasm.

Les finally just sighed, resting against her, panting hard. Lord, she could make him crazy.

"Mmm. I got you, cowboy."

"You do. All over."

Her smile made him happy.

Jesus.

How the hell was he going to make the winter without her if that was what he had to do? He might just freeze without her warm touch. He'd just have to work hard to get her moving fast.

Chapter Twenty

"So, you're going to take the house?"

Les had two more days, and they needed to iron out plans.

"I think I will, yeah. I have no idea what shape it's in." Les had gotten the latest stitches out and had done three days of construction work to earn gas money to go home on.

Of course, he'd also bought her a huge pile of barbecue to last after he was gone and a bottle of darned good wine. Mint chip ice cream and Kleenex too. Turkey.

"Well, I'll talk to the ladies at the library, see if anyone needs catering and all. I'll send what money I can."

Les frowned a bit, blue eyes serious and sure. "I don't want you wearing yourself out, honey."

"I'll need to keep busy." They were curled up on her couch, feeding tidbits to Presley and planning their future. Rosie felt so torn between joy and worry that he would leave and something would change and she'd never see him again. "Pralines aren't all that taxing."

"You do have a talent for it," Les agreed, stroking her back with one big hand. "I could eat a dozen right now."

"Mmm. I'll make you caramels. Am I silly to be so scared?"

Les gave that the thought it deserved, she thought, face screwed up, lips pursed. "No. No, I think this is a huge step. I've never lived with someone, but you have. You know more of what it takes."

"I'm not scared of that part." She whapped his arm. "We did all right in this wee apartment and I know you felt like a caged animal sometimes."

Les laughed. "Well, I am going to get us a big old bed. Yours can go in the guest room."

"I just hope the house has a washer and dryer." And a good stove. So many things to worry about.

"I bet it does. I mean, it used to."

She knew Les' daddy had been the foreman once upon a time. "Did you used to live there?"

"When I was a kid. Once Daddy died we moved into town for a bit. Then I got old enough to cowboy and I moved into the bunkhouse. Not enough hands to have a problem with space anymore."

"I can't wait to see it." A house. She'd make curtains and arrange furniture…

"Oh, honey, how are we gonna wait until spring?" Les kissed her gently, a soft touch of lips that made her feel treasured.

"Because we're practical adults." She felt so much older than she was sometimes. Her relatively short life had been blessed with a lot of adventure. "We know it's better to be prepared."

"Mmm. Just remember that I love you. No matter what."

She chuckled. "That sounds ominous."

"I just know how bad cell reception is up there in the winter pastures. Harris will have your number, though, so if you need to get a hold of me, call and he'll know to answer."

"I can do that." Planning their future. Rosie felt a little awed. "I love you, too."

"That's what makes all the waiting worthwhile." Les hugged her close. "Can we change it to another movie, honey? This one is gonna put me to sleep."

Rosie glanced at the TV, surprised that *Jurassic Park* was done and something with lots of riding in cars was on. "Lord yes. Maybe we should go watch in bed and put the food away."

"Oh, now, that sounds even better."

Rosie laughed, patting his chest. She had a feeling they wouldn't watch much in the way of movies. A man of action could only take so much planning and talking.

She needed to give him something physical to do.

* * * *

"Lester!" His buddy Doug met him at the gas station, trotting over to slap a hand on the hood of his truck. "Wondered if I'd get to say goodbye. We missed you at the last few weekends. Circuit finals are December. You're sitting in eighth place. You ought to hang out until then, make a few more rides."

"Nah." Les found it easier and easier to say no to the rodeo jobs, which meant he'd made the right decision. "Boss in Colorado called. I got the foreman job. I leave tomorrow. I can't even make Waco in October."

"No shit?" Dougie clapped him on the back. "Well good deal. Foreman at twenty-seven. Go you."

"Thanks, buddy."

"What about your lady?"

Les sighed, hating the way they were doing this. "She'll come up in the spring. That way I can fix up the house and she's not wintering right away."

"Then come on back down for Belton. It's only a few weeks off."

"You're pretty persuasive, but I can't."

Doug laughed. "I just hate to see someone waste eighth place."

"I promised Rosie I'd stop rodeoin', Dougie." Might as well say it now that he didn't have to worry about the boys poking at him.

"Shit! Why?"

"She was married to Timmy Cutrer."

Dougie's jaw went slack. "Your girl is Rose Cutrer? Holy hell, man, he bled out in the arena."

"I know. You can pretend to be me if you want."

"Nope. I'm in sixth." Dougie laughed and punched his arm. "Good luck, bro."

"You should come up next summer and see me, ride the Mile High for a bit."

"I might just. I got your number."

Les nodded and waved before going in to pay for his gas, his oil checked, tires inflated. Everything was ready for him to go home but his heart.

Chapter Twenty-One

She wasn't going to cry.

Rose put the last load of Les' clothes in the dryer, then went to package up the caramels for him and check the enchiladas in the oven for supper.

She didn't want to waste their last night doing errands.

And she wasn't going to cry, damn it.

She *wasn't*.

No. She was going to be strong and smile for him and let him know this wasn't goodbye, just so long. He had to cowboy up and go keep his promise to his boss, and she just wasn't sure she could go right now and live in Colorado. Not with winter coming.

She was going to go come spring. She was.

Still, she had support here, close by. A job. Beau within a couple of hours. And asking a girl to come up wasn't like asking her to marry you. She was shacking up, and she wanted to have a decent purse of money saved. Oh, she didn't think Les was gonna leave her high and dry if she went to live with him. He'd make sure she got back home if they…if he… Well. She didn't want to think on that.

This was the smart thing to do, right? Give them some time. Give them some space. Save some money. Plan to get back together in the spring when they knew it was the right thing.

It was grown up.

Smart.

Sort of breaking her heart.

"Hey, honey." Les sounded like one too many cigarettes, though she couldn't smell any on him.

"Hey, cowboy." No crying. None. She had been married to a rodeo cowboy. She knew how to do this long separation thing.

She turned and pushed into his arms and held on tight.

"Mmm. You smell good."

"I probably smell like enchiladas."

"More like burnt sugar and flowers." He grinned. "Caramels and dryer sheets."

"I wanted to get your laundry done, make sure you had caramels to eat on your drive." She traced his smile with her thumb.

"You're good to me, honey." Kissing her fingers, Les pulled her closer.

"I love you. It's how it works."

"I know. I love you, too, Rosie-girl. If I could just stay on, I would. I'll be back come spring to get you."

"I know. I do. This is a good thing. I'll get things settled and stuff."

"There you go." He didn't seem real convinced.

"I'm going to miss you, so much."

"Oh, honey." Finally Les just kissed her, the whole emotional thing obviously getting to him. Such a cowboy.

She might have cried a little bit, but she wasn't stupid about it. Or if she was, Les was decent enough to let her do it. He even danced her around a little, humming an old rodeo song. Silly man. Her silly man.

Rose grinned as Presley started nipping at their heels, barking and bouncing.

"Muttley." Les laughed, shaking his head. "Jealous thing."

"He loves you, cowboy. You're his favorite person."

"He's a doll baby." Les had been so good with Presley. Her baby dog was gonna be inconsolable.

"He is, although I bet your pup misses you, too."

"He's a good boy." There were some great stories about the big doofus, as Les called him.

"I can't wait to meet him."

"Me too. Hell, I can't wait for him to meet Presley." That seemed to tickle him so much.

She nodded. "I'll start hunting for jobs in Steamboat. See what there is."

"Yeah?" *Oh, look at his eyes shine.* "That sounds like good, honey."

"Yeah? I thought so." She met his eyes. "I want to be with you."

"I want that, too. If you can't make it up, I'll come back down. But I still think the boss will have a job for you. And I have the house." Les kissed her again, punctuating his words. Right, like her skiing, snow-loving cowboy would like it here.

He swung her around, mouth still on hers, before letting her go so quick she staggered. "Let me get the mutt a bone."

"Yeah, I need to check the enchiladas..." She turned the oven off, but left them in there to finish.

"Everything good for a bit?" Les shifted from foot to foot, all tense all of a sudden.

"Yeah. Yeah, it just needs a little rest. Are enchiladas okay? You said you liked them best..."

"I love them, honey. I just..." Those wide shoulders lifted. "I want you, Rosie."

"I'm all yours, cowboy." She moved right into his arms.

"That's good to know. I was startin' to hurt." They laughed together and he tugged her into the bedroom, shutting Presley out.

"No hurting." Her fingers pressed again the fly of his jeans. "No hurting my cowboy now."

"No." That big body arched, Les going up on tiptoe. "No, just good stuff."

She undid his belt buckle, fingers protecting his parts as she slid the zipper down. He was hot against the back of her hand, thick and so fine.

"Oh, honey." As if his hand was attached to his zipper, going up as it went down, he reached up to push against her breast, thumb on her nipple. That touch always made her heavy-lidded, her body swaying toward Les' hand. He laughed, the sound low and horny and grand, flicking her nipple again. Even through her tank top, it felt almost too good. Her thighs rubbed together, the tingling starting deep inside her, an itch she needed him to scratch. Or maybe one that Les needed to scratch for her. He was good at that.

His thigh pressed between her legs and she pushed down against it, moaning a little, deep in her throat.

"Feel so good, Rosie." His hands slid back down to her waist to tug at her tank top.

"I do." Her arms went up and she let him get her a little more naked. The fabric fluttered to the floor, and Les bent, drawn to her skin. His mouth was hot as fire.

"H-hungry man." She went up on tiptoe, helping.

"Always." His knee slid up, lifting her on his thigh, and he licked at her nipples.

Her hands landed on his shoulders, her hips rocking, rubbing, back and forth.

"I got you." He murmured it against her skin, his voice muffled a little.

"You so do." The room was starting to spin.

"Come on, honey." They did a little dance, all the way back to the bed. He laid her out, stripping her little shorts off. She felt as if her whole body was flushed, as if she was on fire, as Les stripped off, too, and he was so hard for her, his belly like a board.

Rose licked her lips, moaned a little. Hers.

"So pretty, Rosie." Les crawled up on the bed, moving to cover her.

"You're warm." She loved the way his leg pressed between hers.

"Hot as hell." His cock rubbed on her lower belly, damp at the tip.

She was wet, and her hips couldn't stay still. They had to move, had to slide her sex against Les' muscled thigh. A low groan sounded, Les rocking like he was riding. His balls pressed against her, even, he was moving so hard.

"I... Love..."

His lips wrapped around her nipple, the suction sure, sudden. So good.

His hands slid over her skin, his fingers tugging at her breasts, slipping down to her mound. He was just everywhere. He drove her crazy and she couldn't stop moving, couldn't stop pushing into his hands.

When he spread her legs wide and pushed his cock against her, she was ready. So ready. He slid inside her body like there was nothing else he ever wanted to do. She arched her back and her nipples dragged along his chest as his heavy cock stretched her, started a dull ache in the pit of her belly.

"Damn." Les paused a moment, his forehead against hers. He was breathing hard.

His eyes were so pretty. She kept watching, kept remembering every single inch of him. Then he moved, and she had to close her eyes for just a second. It was too good to keep still, to be able to stay in that moment.

"Cowboy." She was flying. Flying, and the pressure in the pit of her belly just grew.

"Yeah, honey. Look at me." He tilted her chin up with the hand not holding her butt, and suddenly she could look at him again. She loved him—from top to bottom and everywhere else in between. Les loved her right back. She could see it in his eyes, in the hard lines next to his mouth as he fought for control.

She reached out, touched his mouth, loving on his face.

"Rosie." He kissed her fingers.

"Uh-huh." She was going to go crazy with pleasure.

Les changed the angle of his thrusts a tiny bit, and suddenly the friction she needed was right there. *Damn. Oh, damn.* Her lips opened and the muscles in the pit of her belly went tight. Les groaned, the sound rough and deep, from all the way down in his gut. She could feel each sound vibrate against her breasts.

"Love." The word wanted to be a yell, but she couldn't manage it.

"Yes. Oh, honey." He shuddered, his cock moving deep inside her, his hips grinding down. She could feel each wet pulse as he came, could feel his heartbeat.

She held him, moaning through the fading aftershocks of pleasure.

"Sweet Rosie. I swear, you're it for me, girl." He was kind of rambling, not quite coherent.

"Good." She needed to be.

"We'll be all right, honey. I promise."

"We will. Lonely for a few months, but all right." She kissed his nose, smiled. "Love you, cowboy."

"I love you, too, Rosie." He'd never had any trouble saying it to her. Timmy hadn't either. Cowboys got a bad rap for that sometimes, and they didn't always deserve it.

She nodded, let herself rest with him a minute, let herself hold on tight.

Chapter Twenty-Two

Rosie pulled into the long drive and honked, just in case the pack was out and loose. Beau's hounds weren't mean, but they were big and there were a lot of them. A whole lot. And they were *drooly*.

Mr. Sam was the one who came out of the house, and he pulled a big male bloodhound away from her driver's side window, smiling at her. "Rosalie! How ya? How are you?"

The poor man, since he'd been so hurt, talking wasn't his friend.

"Mr. Sam. I... Are y'all busy?" She'd called and said she was coming, but it was always good to make sure.

"No. Beau is cooking." Seeing her look, he laughed. "Jambalaya. He made it mild."

"Oh, yum. I brought pralines and divinity." She wouldn't make caramels until she got to her cowboy.

"Hooee." Sam opened the door for her, helping her out with one hand. "Come on."

She took his hand, kissed his cheek, and handed him the candy. The man seemed so good, so happy. There'd been that little bit where they all thought they'd lose him, but now... She'd never seen Sam Bell look so healthy. Especially since he had a hat on and she couldn't see his scars.

They chatted a bit on the way in, Sam haltingly telling her about the puppies and the new shed.

She oohed and aahed, admiring Beau's new truck and the neat front porch deal they'd built. "Y'all have been busy."

"We have, huh?" He opened the back door, and Beau was there in the kitchen, grinning at her.

"Hey, Miss Rose."

"Beau!" He opened his arms and she got her hug. "Oh, God. I've missed y'all something fierce."

"Well, it's good to see you. We love having you about, you know that." Before she could blink she had a cup of coffee and a seat at the table and some amazing pie thing that had to be from Beau's long-suffering granny.

"Thank you." She dug in, humming over the sweet. "Lord, this is good. So, y'all are doing good?"

God, she wanted to tell them about Les.

"We're doing just fine." Beau had sat across from her, and he was staring. Hard.

"What?" She knew she was blushing.

"You got something on your mind, Miss Rose. You might as well tell us what."

"I'm going to Colorado. I love him and he loves me and he doesn't know I'm coming, because I want to surprise him, but I'm going. In ten days. I'm going to go. I wasn't supposed to go until spring, but I can't wait." She just blurted it out.

Beau sat back, glancing at Sam, who nodded, one eyebrow up. "This that Les feller?"

"Yeah. I… You don't think it's wrong, do you? I loved Timmy, you know that, but…" She wasn't dead, too. She had to grasp this with both hands.

"No, ma'am. If he's a stand-up guy, I think you deserve him, and to be happy." Beau smiled, the expression lighting up his eyes.

"He's wonderful and I was going to wait, but… Mister Beau, I miss him. I miss him every day."

"Well, now." Beau and Sam shared another look, this one a smile. "Then you ought to go. If he has a place for you there."

"If he doesn't, I'll get a baby apartment like I have here." She'd been hunting and, Lord, those tiny places were pricey, but that was okay. It was.

She was frugal.

"Well, if you need anything, you holler, you hear? You're family. We won't let you go wrong." Beau reached out to pat her hand.

"No. No, you wouldn't." She grabbed his fingers. "I love him, Beau. I want to have his babies. Is that nuts?"

"No. No, it ain't crazy." Beau held on, just smiling at her. He seemed happy for her. For real. "Love is a funny thing."

"Yeah. Yeah, I guess it is." She couldn't fight her grin.

"You know, I ain't heard much about this guy." Sam sat down, too, leaning back and looking like he was about to grill her.

"He's a working cowboy. Rode a little on the bulls, but he did broncs at the big shows."

"No shit?" Sam grunted when Beau's foot connected with his under the table. "Pardon my French."

She chuckled, grinned. "Yes, sir. I…I saw him ride the once, he did good." Then she winked. "He's awful tall for a bull rider."

They both cackled, not being tall fellers. "Well, we know a few, huh?"

"A couple. He's got four inches on AJ Gardner." Wait, did that sound dirty?

"Well, now." Beau's eyes twinkled, and he chuckled. Okay, so it had sounded risqué.

"Hush, you. Missy'd pluck me bald-headed for even thinking that and y'all know it."

"She would." They cackled like a pair of old hens. "So, this boy lives where again?"

"Colorado. In the mountains. Steamboat Springs." It was like a ski place, way up high. She'd been reading on it.

"That sounds fun." Sam was a good soul. She could tell he was tickled for her, where Beau was happy but worried.

"I've been real careful with Timmy's insurance and with saving the last month or two. I can make it a year without a job, maybe longer."

"Sounds like you've really thought all this through." Beau got up to stir his jambalaya and get her more coffee. "You'll have to let me and Sam look at your truck. Make sure it will hold to the weather driving up there.

"I'd appreciate that, Mister Beau. I want to get there and surprise him, be settled in time to make him Thanksgiving supper."

"That sounds like fun." He patted her shoulder, and it wasn't a bit condescending. "You'll have to give me his number up there, just in case."

"Surely. That way you can always find me." Beau Lafitte was her family, he had her back, and she had his.

"You know it. We can come skiing."

BA Tortuga

They got to talking after that, just all about the families and all. It was a fine thing.

By the time the sun was fixin' to set, she was feeling a little wore. "I've got a drive home, y'all."

"No one will talk if you spend the night here, Miss Rose." Putting a hand on her shoulder, Beau squeezed a little. "I don't want you driving in the dark."

"You sure you don't mind?" Presley was still outside, chasing the bloodhounds, really playing hard. She usually had him on a leash but at Beau's she never had to worry. Those hounds protected her baby.

"Not a bit. You need to eat with us, anyway. Beau will pout." Sam headed outside to gather up her little overnight bag. Living with a rodeo cowboy, she'd learned to always have one packed.

"I was wondering if you might come help me pack my baby truck on the first. It's a long drive and I'm thinking about buying a little hardtop to keep my things safe."

"Sure." Nodding, Beau puttered around, getting out plates and all. He seemed good, too. Happy.

"Retirement suits you."

"Thank you." That smile went all the way to his eyes, warming them up so much. "I never thought I'd like it this much, but I sure do."

"Yeah? Y'all have been busy since." What with the dogs and the TV and appearances and cattle.

"We have. Been working, but not so hard that Sammy gets messed up, huh?" The cornbread came out of the oven, smelling like heaven. Beau could cook, no matter what everyone thought.

"I think it looks good on both of you." God, she missed Les.

160

Beau gave her a spontaneous hug, which seemed to surprise him as much as it did her. "We'll miss you being close."

"You'll come visit. I'll come home to see y'all." She had to go.

"I know. We won't let you get away that easy."

"I hope not." She grinned, nodded to Sam. "I don't know what I'd've done without y'all."

"You'd best invite us to the wedding," Sam said, which put the first doubt in her mind, because with all their planning, Les had never mentioned marriage.

"If he asks. We haven't talked on it." She shrugged, hugging on herself a little bit. "I mean, y'all know me and Timmy didn't have babies. He might want to make sure I could, first." She wasn't stupid. Cowboys loved babies.

"We always kinda figured it was Timmy." Beau's cheeks went fiery red. "It happens to roughstock cowboys sometimes."

"That... Well, the doctors then said that I was good, but...I'm older now."

"Oh. Oh! Well, you still have a lot of good years. You're not even thirty. Look at Missy Gardner."

"Yeah. She can catch pregnant if Aje walks through the room with a boner." She blinked, then laughed right out loud. God, she hadn't said something like that since before she lost Timmy.

Sam and Beau blinked too. Then they hooted, both of them laughing so hard that the dogs set to howling outside.

They all laughed until she was sore, then she grinned at her friends. "I'll make us some coffee and we can have candy in the front room, if y'all want."

"That sounds like a plan, Miss Rose." Beau nodded, and Sam grinned, and it was all good.

She could only hope going to see Les turned out as well.

Chapter Twenty-Three

The phone rang just as Les and Iggy were settling in with a DVD and a beer. Well, Iggy had a rawhide, not a beer, but still. His heart kicked into high gear, and Les hopped up to answer. Maybe it was Rosie. He loved it when she called. "'Lo?"

"This Les Jacoby?"

Not Rose. Some male voice he didn't know. "Yeah. This is Les. How can I help you?"

"Les, this is Beau Lafitte, Rose's friend."

"Well, hey." Beau. Lafitte. Lord. Only one of the best bull riders ever.

"Hey. Rose came by yesterday, spent the night here. She... She's got good things to say for you."

"Does she?" Les grinned a little. Rose had told him about Beau and his traveling partner, so he wasn't jealous. "Well, I sure am glad to hear that."

"Yessir. I... Well, I don't want to step on any toes, now, but I reckon I'm the only thing she's got to family and I think you and me oughta talk."

It actually did him good to hear someone say that. It made him happy that Rosie had someone in her corner. Still, why she'd gone to see Beau was a mystery.

"Surely. Have I done something I don't know about?"

"No, sir. She's fixin' to do something you don't know about." Beau took a deep breath, and Les heard another male voice telling him to get on with it.

"Is she?" What the hell? Was she gonna break up with him?

"Yup. She's packing her truck up, coming up there to surprise you. I wouldn't spoil her surprise, normally, but…"

"Packing her…" Les shorted out a little, the joy kinda overwhelming. Rosie was going to surprise him.

"Yeah. Yeah, and if you don't want her up there, man, tell me now. You let her drive all that way by herself and then turn her away and you'll have a bunch of cowboys coming to beat your ass."

"No. No, I won't do that." Oh, god. This was really happening. Les couldn't be more tickled. "I been working on the house. I even did up the extra bath in roses."

"Oh." He heard a soft little chuckle. "Poot, he's fixing her up a house."

"Fucking A! Go Rose!"

Les laughed, just feeling it well up in his chest.

"She's leaving here on the first. Bringing her dog and a truckload."

"Oh. Oh, that's…" The first of November. Shit. That could be dangerous. "I—is she gonna be checking in with you? It could be snowing already, time she comes across."

"She is. She's a smart girl and she's all fluttery about surprising you, but…well, that's a big damn surprise."

"It is." He might have dropped dead if she'd just shown up without him having any warning. That would have been bad. "You'll keep in touch with me as she comes, yeah? That way I won't be tempted to call her every five minutes."

"You got my word, man. You are intending on marrying her, right? 'Cause she's not the shaking-up kind of lady."

"I know. I am." He hadn't asked before he left because, well, what if she hated Colorado? What if he'd gotten killed over the winter, working the cattle? What about a ring? He'd wanted to wait until spring to ask, just in case.

"Good." He thought that was satisfaction in Beau Lafitte's voice. "She's a good girl. You're lucky. She... Well, you oughta know. She's thinkin' you ain't asked 'cause she didn't catch pregnant with her first husband."

"Oh. No. No, I mean I knew it was him. She mentioned it once." Les rolled his eyes. Rosie was a dork. "I mean, she went on the pill with me, so I knew..."

"Yeah. Yeah. I just thought the information might help. Remember now, though, you don't know nothing."

"Right." Shit, he was talking to a total stranger about having sex with Rosie.

"Congrats, man. You got my number now, if you need it."

Shit. Shit, he was talking to the three-million-dollar cowboy, who was treating him like family. When had this become his life?

"Thanks." He actually had to clear his throat a little. "I—thanks. I'll treat her right."

"You better. I'll see you at the wedding, if not before. Keep me informed, man."

"I will. Thanks for letting me know." If he'd lost Rosie on the road somewhere... God.

"You got it. Night, man."

"Goodnight." Les hung up, with Beau Lafitte for God's sake, and resisted the urge to call Rosie right off. She'd know from his voice that something was up.

Of course, it wasn't a second later and his phone rang again. He *knew* it was her. Les took a deep breath, trying for normal. "Hello?"

"Hey, cowboy." Rosie sounded tired, but good. "How's it going?"

"Good. How are you, honey?" It was so good to hear her voice, one way or the other.

"Pooped. Did a lot today. Missing you."

"What are you up to?" He bit his lip, holding in the string of questions he really wanted to ask.

"Cleaning. I went to see Sam and Beau yesterday and ended up spending the night at the ranch."

"Did you? How are they doing?" He had to really push it, because he felt like he was lying to her.

"Good. Happy. I had fun. Did you get the caramels I mailed you?"

"I did. Thank you, honey." He'd tried to email her about them, but he was never sure if that electronic shit went through from his satellite Internet. Texts were just as bad.

"Good." He heard her sigh and heard the couch groan as she flopped. "We're getting all the Halloween decorations ready for the library."

"Yeah? The kids excited?" He was... God, she was coming up on the first. He needed to clean. Get that kitchen cabinet project done.

"You know it. You have to be so careful not to make the older ones frustrated, the younger ones scared. I have a gypsy costume."

"Got your crystal ball?" Les settled back down on the couch, stroking Iggy's ears. No sense pacing.

"Long skirt, lots of costume jewelry, and a scarf in my hair."

"You'll have to send me pictures, honey." That they had down. Les was way better with his cell phone than he was with the old computer.

"I will." Presley was barking in the background. "I'm having the house phone turned off, just to save the pennies. I'll keep my cell, though."

"Okay." Les paused, then went ahead and asked. "Do you need me to wire you some money, hon? Just in case?"

"No. No, you keep your money, love. I'll be fine. I have money in the bank, I just like to have a nice cushion, in case."

"Yeah." Les had been surprised at how much he had banked since he'd taken on the foreman job. The boss was letting him have the house as a comp, hoping to keep him on, and the renovations were going along pretty cheap. Folks down in town had been generous, once they heard he was wanting to bring up a fiancée from Texas.

He grinned at himself. Shit, it was like they'd all decided, if he was bringing a woman, he was staying permanent instead of haring off to rodeo all the time.

Les guessed that wasn't far off.

Hot damn. "Well, I sure do miss you, girl. Been working hard, trying to keep busy so I don't call you at work."

"I miss you, too. Bad." She chuckled. "You know, this is why I don't fall for cowboys."

The familiar tease was gentle, sweet and made him smile.

"I know, honey. We just have another few months, right?" Not even that, but he couldn't let on.

"I know. I'm good, just pouting, maybe a little hormonal."

"Oh." He grinned some more. "Well, have some chocolate and think about us making out like fools."

"Mmm. Chocolate. I bought Oreos at the store."

"Oh, that sounds good." He had a ham sandwich in the fridge, and a piece of carrot cake from up at the house.

"Uh-huh. I keep thinking I'll make enchiladas, but that's a lot of work for one. Maybe I'll make tamales at Christmas, though."

"Oh, that would be good. Hell, if I could I'd come down."

"I know. Maybe... Maybe I could come up." *Sweet girl.*

"Oh. Do you get time off at the library, honey? I could get us a little tree..." That just. Damn. He was gonna have Thanksgiving with her too. Shit fire.

"How fun would that be?" God, she sounded happy, tickled.

"That would be real good, honey. They do pretty things up here too. Lights and all. Hayrides."

"Yeah? Will there be snow, do you think? I've never seen snow at Christmas."

"Ought to be." There might well be snow before she got there. He couldn't even tell her to get chains, because anyone just coming up for Christmas would fly into Denver.

"Neat." They talked for a little longer, then she sighed. "I'd better let you sleep. I'll call you tomorrow night, if you're not busy?"

She asked, every night.

"I'm not planning on ever being too busy for you, Rosie-girl." He said the same thing every night too. "I love you, honey."

"Love you, cowboy. Sweet dreams."

The phone went dead and he grinned. He thought he would have the best dreams ever.

Chapter Twenty-Four

"The top's okay, right? You think it's okay?" She looked at Mr. Beau, hands shaking. She'd sold her furniture, packed her truck with her clothes, her movies and books, and her whole kitchen. She needed that stuff to make candy.

She was doing this.

She was.

God help her.

"Yes, ma'am. Sam made sure of it." Beau and Sam had come down to help her. They were even going to store her rocking chair until she could afford to ship it.

"You think he's going to be happy?" Was she doing the right thing?

"I think he'll be over the moon." Beau patted her shoulder. "Any man would be lucky to have you."

"Yeah?" She looked at him, then pushed into his arms. "I'm sorta scared, Mr. Beau."

"I know." He hugged her tight-tight and kissed her cheek. All cowboys had a certain scent to them — leather and smell good and work. It was comforting.

"I'm heading to Little Rock to see Jeannie and Mark, then Carrie and Jackson in Springfield, and Lisa and Little Joe in Topeka. It'll take a couple extra days, but I want to visit." She had riders to see in Lincoln and Cheyenne too. It would be an adventure. Kinda going around her elbow to get to her ass, but it would work.

"You call me every step of the way." He stared at her hard, like her daddy would have. "Sam and I have that extra plane ticket we talked on. We can fly in anywhere and drive you the rest of the way."

"Okay. Yeah. I'm good. I promise. I'll miss y'all." So bad. They were good friends.

"We'll be in touch."

Sam chuckled, coming over, wiping his hands on a rag. "Your oil is fine, honey."

"Okay. I have new tires. I have my emergency money, my phone." She had a clean pair of jeans and all sorts of layers in the cab.

"You're on your way." Beau hugged her again, close. "You've got people, Miss Rose. Don't you forget it."

"Never. You don't forget about me, either, huh?"

"Not a chance." Beau finally kissed her cheek and stepped back, letting Sam envelop her in a big old hug.

"Okay. Okay, I'm off. I'll call from Little Rock tonight. Promise." Maybe Texarkana. The day was slipping by...

"You get on the road and don't look back, Rose." Beau actually patted her butt, which made her giggle madly.

"I will. I will." She glanced at Presley, took a deep breath. She could do this.

She could.

Really.

She hoped.

* * * *

Les sat by the phone, waiting for Rosie to call.

Lord, but this was a nail-biter, knowing his girl was on the road by herself. He spent the evenings chewing his nails until she called, because then he knew she was somewhere safe.

The phone rang, her number popping up. "Hey, cowboy."

Jesus, she sounded tired.

"Hey, honey. I'm missing you."

"Me too." He heard her sigh, wondered if she'd made it as far as she'd hoped.

"How was your day, Rosie?" He tried to keep it normal. Tried hard.

"Long. A little scary. I went somewhere to eat I'd never been before and I didn't like it."

"Yeah? Was it nasty?" Poor baby. If someone had been awful to her, he might have to go kill them.

"Yeah. It was kinda... I was just a little scared, I guess. I'm such a dork."

"Well, you're a stud, honey." He grinned at himself. She was something else.

"That's me. Little Miss Studly." He could hear Presley in the background, yapping. "Oh, Pres. Hush. Just rest. Tell me about your day, cowboy."

"Give him one of them pepperoni sticks, honey." Surely she'd brought some with her. "I moved a bunch of cows today, did some feeding." He'd damned near cut his hand off on a piece of wire but he wasn't about to tell her that. She would freak out.

"Yeah? I think we should invest in a brood mare for you, breed some babies."

"You think so?" Oh, now. That was a thought. A real thought. Les liked the idea of maybe breeding bucking horses. "I like it."

"I do. We need a nest egg, something to build on, huh?" She was so damn smart. And his.

"We do. I think it's a grand idea. I can ask around, and maybe when you come up for Christmas, we can go look at some fillies."

"That would be fun, huh?" He heard her sigh, sniffle a wee bit. "Miss you."

"I miss you, too. You sound like it was a purely bad day, Rosie. What can I do?" He held his breath, half hoping she'd say what was what.

"Tell me that you love me a little?"

"I love you more than a little, honey. I love you this big." He knew she couldn't see, but the first time he'd done that, she'd teased him about his long arms.

Oh, Lord. He did adore that happy little laugh.

"That help any?" He sure hoped so. His girl didn't need to carry such a heavy load alone.

"It helped a lot." She laughed again, sounding happier for sure.

"Good. I don't want you sad, Rosie-girl." Or hurting or too tired to go on.

"Thank you, cowboy. I'll talk to you tomorrow?"

"Of course you will. I'll be here, waiting." Waiting for her to come home safe to him, to tell him she was only miles away.

"Okay, love. I'll talk to you tomorrow. Night."

"You know it, honey. I love you." He was getting downright unhappy about this whole traveling thing, too.

Still, she had to show up soon, right?

She had to.

He was gonna go crazy if she didn't.

Chapter Twenty-Five

Rose hit Beau Lafitte's number on her cell, chin on her knees. *Please be home. Please answer.*

Please.

"'Lo?"

Oh, thank God. And it was Beau, not Sam.

"Beau? It's Rose." Just like that, she started crying. God damn it. She'd been doing so good too.

"Miss Rose? Oh, honey, what's wrong?" Beau's voice sounded like home, so comforting, the slow drawl a balm.

"It's dark and scary and I blew a tire. I'm waiting for Triple A, but it's just... It's real dark out here and I'm so tired and things just aren't going easy." Something had gone wrong every day, it seemed, and the five-day trip had become ten when her truck broke down in Omaha and she was so tired.

"You what? Where are you? Sam and I can be there in no time."

"Wyoming. It's cold and yucky and the truck's not doing so good." It felt so right, just to let it go, just to fess up and talk.

"Rose, you need to call Les. Hell, he could be there in an hour or two." Beau sounded so sympathetic that it made her tear up again.

"No. No, I just have to be strong and I can be there tomorrow. It's just… It's real dark and I can't call him because I'll cry."

"Well, if you need me to come, I can. Or if you just need me to sit here and chat, I can do that, too."

"I just… Can we talk, Beau? Just until the guy comes? I'm sorta scared." Scared and cold and feeling like the world's biggest idiot. Her tires were new, damn it, and she'd hit a two by four in the road and boom.

"We can. Are you in the car with the doors locked? That will make you feel better." He rambled on about things she could do to feel safe and warm that wouldn't run down the battery.

She started to relax, to breathe. "You're my best friend."

She felt like she could make it now.

"Well, that's good to know. I love you to death, Miss Rose. I don't want you to be scared or nothin'."

"This is harder than I thought. I'm feeling like a weenie."

"You're doin' fine." When she made a protesting noise, he hushed her. "You are. You're not used to any of this, and you're powering through. I'm proud."

"You think Les'll be excited? You think he'll be happy?" If she got there and he didn't want her, Rose thought she might just die.

"I think any man who wasn't would be a fool. You said he didn't want to leave you behind, right?"

"He didn't. He wanted me to come along. I was the one to be all adult and say we needed to wait."

"There you go. He's got it bad for you, Miss Rose. Don't you forget it."

"I'm trying, Mister Beau. I swear. I just... I'm real tired. I'll be with him tomorrow, though, won't I?"

"You will. You surely will." The certainty in Beau's voice might just carry her through. That and the headlights of the tow truck.

"They're here." Thank God. "Thank you, honey. I'll text you when I get to a hotel. There's a La Quinta I'm going to crash at."

"Good girl. If you have any more trouble, though, you call. You hear?"

"I promise. Thank you." She hung up after goodbyeing him and got out of the car, hushing Presley. Tomorrow.

Tomorrow she'd be in Les' arms.

Please God.

* * * *

Les limped into his kitchen, debating between water and a cup of coffee. He'd left himself a Thermos full this morning, before the snow got so bad and he had to get out there and bring in the calves from the spring. The poor babies would freeze to death in this kind of monster blizzard. They weren't even yearlings yet.

He'd tugged off his boots by the back door, and the floor felt cold under his socks, so Les went with coffee. He poured a cup, then grabbed his phone where he'd left it plugged in on the counter. There wasn't a bit of sense in taking it out in this shit — he wouldn't have any bars and he'd just lose the damn thing anyway, get it wet as hell.

He thought maybe his hair was steaming. He flipped to the missed calls, and he had ten from Beau Lafitte. Shit. His heart kicked into overdrive, and he didn't waste time listening to voice mails. He called right back, needing to hear whatever it was from the horse's mouth.

"'Lo?" That wasn't Beau.

"Uh, this is Les Jacoby. I need to speak to Beau."

"Ah. I'm Sam. Rosie hurt the tires in her truck." The man was hard to hear and not making a bit of sense.

"What?" She had a flat? "Is she at a hotel? We're having bad storms. She can stay where she is until it blows over."

"'Kay. I'll call her. Wait there, huh?"

"I will." Waiting. Jesus. He wasn't supposed to know she was coming but Les wanted to call now.

He rapped his fingers on the counter, fed the dog, waiting for the damn phone to ring. When it finally did, he tapped answer right away, barking his hello.

"Hey, Les. I can't get hold of her. I haven't been able to since last night. She was waiting on Triple A and said they were there, but that was the last." Beau sounded so damned worried.

"Where was she?"

"Wyoming—near Laramie, I think."

"Fuck." Panic rose in his throat because the weather was vicious all over their region. "I have to go get her."

"Good. Good, is it pretty much a straight shot?"

"Well, it wouldn't be tough if the weather wasn't a bear."

"Yeah. Well, me and Sammy can start up your way."

Because *that* would help. Les shook his head. "No. No, I'll head her way and keep calling."

"Let me know when you get to her, will you?" Beau was a good man and Les would be so tickled to meet him at the wedding.

"I'll keep you posted. Sorry, I was out gathering calves or I would have been on it earlier."

"Damn, man. You mean you actually work for a living?" The tease made him breathe again, the laugh surprising him.

"I know, right? Thanks for everything, Beau." He needed to get moving, try to call his girl.

He started yanking on his coat again, as he dialed Rose up. The damn thing went straight to voice mail. "Call me as soon as you can, honey," he said before hanging up and calling the boss.

"Les, 'sup?"

"I have to go to Laramie, boss. Just to pick up my girl."

"There's no way, son. Highway patrol's closed both 14 and 125. They aren't letting anyone through." Harris sounded as bushed as he felt.

"God *damn* it!" He slammed his hand onto the kitchen counter.

"I know." The boss sighed. "I have a cousin up that way if you want me to call."

"I don't even know where she is, boss. I mean, she was outside of Laramie, last I knew."

"Why in the living hell would she go through Wyoming from Texas to come here?"

"Something about mountains and a Cajun giving advice." Really, it had been about staying with friends instead of hotels and her truck breaking down and her wanting to avoid that road between I70 and Steamboat.

"Oh, for fuck's sake."

Yeah. Yeah, and now he felt like an idiot, going along with this stupid game of hers. What if she was hurt? Lost? His Rosie was from goddamn New Orleans for goodness sake and her people had all died in a storm that folks knew was coming.

Les took a deep breath. "If you don't mind calling your cousin, I'd love to have someone on tap. I'll try her line again."

"Good deal. Hang tight, huh? She'll be here soon."

Les hung up with the boss and went to flip on his shortwave to get the news from the National Weather Service. Okay, he had chains for his truck, had emergency gear. As soon as he could leave, he would.

He tried Rosie again and got nothing. "Come on, Rosie girl. Call me back. I'm thinking of you."

Les couldn't feel less helpless, and that was an idea he wasn't used to.

One way or the other, he sure as shit didn't intend to get used to it now.

Chapter Twenty-Six

Rose sat in the parking lot of this truck stop outside of Laramie, and sobbed, head down on her steering wheel.

She couldn't do this. She just couldn't. It was scary and roads were closed everywhere. She couldn't call Mr. Beau and, even worse, she couldn't call Les or get her GPS to work because there wasn't any signal here.

She couldn't go back and she couldn't go forward and Presley was crying and…

The knock to her window scared the peewaddin' out of her, and she let out a sharp scream, finding this short, squat muscled woman in a flannel shirt and a huge open coat standing there when she glanced up.

She lowered her window a crack. "Can… Can I help you?"

"Well, sweetpea, I was fixin' to ask you that very same question." The voice was warm, deep, and absolutely from back home somewhere. The woman had bright blue eyes and a gold tooth, which made Rose want to burst into hysterical giggles.

"I'm trying to get to Steamboat Springs—have you ever heard of it? I'm meeting my boyfriend there, but there's no signal and I'm... I'm..."

The tears started again, hard and absolutely unavoidable.

"Hey. Hey, come on. Let's get a cup of joe, yeah? Bring the pup. Janie won't mind and it's dead in there."

She almost said no, but the lights at the truck stop glowed warm and she was just freaking out. Sniffing, she wrapped her scarf tighter, then tucked Presley into his little carrier. The cold took her breath when she stepped out.

"I'm Charlene." The lady steadied her, one hand under her arm.

"Rose. Rose Cutrer."

"Pleased. Come on, now. Let's warm you up and find a plan."

She followed along, feeling as if she was on another planet. Everything looked like the surface of the moon, and she watched steam rise off Charlene's shoulders when they made it inside.

"Oh, Lord. Hey, Charlene. Who's your friend?"

"Name's Rose. She's heading to Steamboat with no chains and Texas plates."

"Oh, poor baby!" The waitress wore a name tag that read Janie, so maybe she was the owner or manager too. "I bet you swung up this way to avoid bad weather, huh? This sure is a freak thing."

"I did. I was trying to avoid the big mountain passes, you know? It's still ninety degrees at home." A freak thing? For real? God, that made her feel like less of an idiot.

"Usually not until Thanksgiving at the earliest. Sit. You look peaked."

"I am." She put Presley down beside her. "Is there coffee? I'd kill for a good cup."

"Well, maybe not good," Charlene said.

"Hey! Don't make me hurt you, you old dyke."

Rose gasped and stared up, eyes wide, but Janie was laughing and so was her new friend.

"Two coffees and I want a patty melt and then feed this poor girl something warm."

"I have a green chile stew or potato soup, or the special is meatloaf and mashed potatoes."

"Green chile stew sounds amazing. Thank you."

Janie headed into the tiny kitchen and Charlene gave her a long once over. "Okay, then. You're heading into Steamboat, you said?"

"Yes, ma'am."

"Do you have chains for your truck?"

She didn't even know what that meant, so Rosie shook her head. Presley wiggled and she put him on the seat between her and the wall.

"They go on your tires," Charlene said. "Give you traction."

"Oh. No. Can I...? Where do they do that?" Was there a Wal-Mart close?

"Oh, I always carry a few sets." Charlene grinned, that tooth glinting. "People slide off the road and stuff and I try to help out."

"Oh, for real? I can totally, like, pay for them. I just..." The tears started again and suddenly Janie was beside her and there were three coffees and a fifth of Jack.

"The roads are closed, honey. Least until the ice lets up, but we have heat and food, even if the lights go out." Janie put a shot in all their glasses. "Now, tell us what the hell you're doing so far outside of the Lone Star state."

BA Tortuga

The coffee burned, all the way down, and by the time the patty melt had cooked, Rose had told them about Les and Timmy, about Beau and Sam and her crazy plan to come up here and surprise her cowboy.

The green chile stew was hot and spicy and tasted like heaven, if heaven was a truck stop in Wyoming.

* * * *

Les slammed the door of his truck, cursing a blue streak. The roads were... Well, he couldn't make it off the ranch. He had to round up enough hands to do extra feeding or the cattle would freeze.

He was going out of his mind with worry.

It had been more than a day since he'd heard from her. More than a day since anyone had and she didn't know shit about driving on snow.

Oh, God. Let her get here safe.

Les whistled up Izzy, knowing he had work to do. He hated to play this game, but life went on and the ranch didn't wait.

There was nothing he could do that wouldn't make shit worse.

Harris came to him, bundled up nice and good. "You hear anything yet?"

"No, sir."

"I've got a call out on the CB, Les. The truckers are hunting for her. So's my cousin."

"Thank you. I should have gone to get her as soon as Mr. Beau called me the first time. What was I thinking?"

"Oh, son. You're a man in love. There ain't been one of us that has ever thought in that situation."

"She was so proud of surprising me, I reckon. I wanted to work on the house and surprise her, too."

"Well, just think how good it'll be when all's said and done. My missus is excited to meet her. I'm excited that means you'll stay."

"I will." He smiled because the boss deserved it for that. "I appreciate all your help."

"You're family. I'll holler if I hear anything. You take the boys and get those calves in."

"Yessir." They'd get the hot feed out and round up the rest of the calves. Mommas too if they could.

Maybe by the time he was done, the ice would cut the hell out and he could go find his Rosie.

Chapter Twenty-Seven

Rose swerved on the highway, her heart slamming in her chest.

There was snow.

Everywhere.

Snow.

And it wouldn't stop and it wouldn't stop and she couldn't bear doing this one more minute, even with all the help she'd been getting.

She'd never been so fucking scared.

Never.

The ice had moved out and the snow had started overnight as they'd slept at the truck stop. The white stuff was heavy and wet, big flakes that made everything slick as snot. So frightening. Her hands hurt, her shoulders hurt. Her head was killing her. The light was impossible, visibility was down to nothing, and all she could see were Charlene's taillights on her Safeway trailer. They were crawling along, her eyes feeling like grit stuck in them. She almost missed it when Charlene's turn signal came on.

She slid a little because she pushed the brakes too hard, but she kept it on the road. Just barely. Rose pulled into a truck stop and slid to a stop beside Charlene's semi. Her own personal little hero hopped out, smiled at her, gold tooth glinting. "Okay. We gotta stop, honey. They've closed my route and I'm going to cool my heels here for a little bit of time. You're in Steamboat, though. You know where you're going?"

"Yeah." Kinda.

Except not really.

Still, Charlene had been a life saver, had put her chains on, had babied her and her wee truck all the way here.

"You've been a doll baby." She hopped out of her truck, hugged Charlene hard. "Thank you."

"Honey, let me give you my spare coat? That wee jacket you have is not gonna work."

"Oh, I couldn't..."

"Bullshit. You're heading where?"

"The Rocking D Ranch."

"Good deal." Charlene grabbed a huge quilted jacket out of her truck and shoved it at her. "Go on. It's gonna get worse. You be careful, pretty girl."

"I will. I promise." She took a deep, deep breath. Then she got back in the truck and grabbed her little map.

Charlene tapped on the truck window.

"Hey! Come on. One more cup of coffee."

"But you said..."

"Yeah, but you're looking tired. One cup."

"I. Yeah. Yeah, okay. One cup. You think Presley'll be okay?"

"Pop him in the little carrier this time. No one here will bitch, sweetpea."

"Okay."

Okay.

One more cup of coffee before she did the most frightening thing in her whole life. Alone.

* * * *

The phone rang at three in the afternoon, and Les lunged for it, his stomach rolling. Every time the phone rang, he knew something awful had happened and someone was finally going to tell him.

"Yeah?"

"Les? Sallie. Man, you gotta come down to the café."

"Sallie, I'm a little busy." Waiting on his southern girl in a blizzard.

"Les. You gotta come. Now." He'd known Sallie for years, and she never did anything without a reason.

"What's going on?" He'd come help if someone was in trouble, but if it was a moose at the truck stop, he needed to stay and wait for Rosie. The snow had come again overnight. All ten inches and still snowing.

Sallie's voice dropped. "Les, your lady's here. Charlene stops here every week and she says your girl can't go no further."

"What?" Oh, shit and shinola. She was there. In town. "I'll be there. Keep her in that café."

"Good. She looks wiped, honey."

"I'm on my way. Just... Don't give her the bill or something." He could be there in maybe twenty.

"You got it." The phone line went dead, and Les grabbed his coat and his keys, heading out like his ass was on fire.

The snow was coming down, just vicious, and he couldn't help but be fiercely proud of his girl. She was so brave. So smart. Yeah. He was proud. Now it was time to go get her, though. Maybe kick her ass a little.

His phone rang as he got into the truck, Rosie's ringtone sounding.

"Hello?" His heart just pounded in his chest.

"Les? Les, are you busy? I need to talk to you." She was crying—he could hear it.

"No, honey. I'm right here." *Please don't tell me you want to go home to Texas*, he thought. *Please.*

"I... I wanted to surprise you, so much, but I'm cold and I'm scared and I need you to come help me. I tried to surprise you, but..." She sniffled, sobbed. "I'm here, in Colorado. In Steamboat. I missed you, so bad."

"Oh, honey. Where? I can be in town in fifteen minutes." Since he was already in his truck and heading out, it would be no problem.

"You're not mad?"

"God, no. I'm tickled. Snow's bad, though, huh?" He got out on the main road, giving it as much speed as he dared with the chains for traction.

"Uh-huh. I tried to make it the whole way, but..."

"Oh, Rosie. You did so good. This is a freak storm."

"I'm at the...uh. Jack's Truck Stop. Me and Presley."

"I'm on my way, honey. Which way did you come up? From Denver or Laramie?"

"Laramie. Do... Do I need to get me a hotel room or something?"

"No, honey. No. I'll come in and get you, and we'll get someone else to drive your truck in to the ranch." Someone would do it for him.

"You're coming? For real?" She was just about to lose her shit—he could hear it in her voice.

"I am. I'm ten minutes away." Provided he didn't slide off the road.

"Okay. You be careful. I'll pay my tab and stuff." She sniffled again. "I love you, huh?"

"Oh, Rosie. My girl. You came for me." He was so proud he could bust.

"I did. I couldn't wait anymore to be home with you."

"I could just explode, Rosie-girl." He chuckled. "You know I been missing Presley."

"He misses you. Come fetch me home, cowboy. I need to lay my burden down a while."

He could see the lights of the truck stop through the thick snow, now, and Les nodded. "I'm almost there, lady. Get your huggin' arms ready."

He hung up the phone, parked by her tiny little truck that was loaded up with her things. Lord. She came out, Presley's carrier in one hand, so Les hopped out of his truck and hustled over, grabbing her in a bear hug even as he took the carrier from her. "Oh, honey."

"Les." Those great big eyes met his and filled with tears. "You're here."

"I am. Hi, honey." He kissed her, and her nose was so cold. So cold even after she'd been in the café.

She shivered and snuggled in. "Hi. Hi, Les."

"Hey. You feel good." Presley was going crazy, yapping like a fool.

"Is... Is there somewhere we could go?" she asked. "I don't want to intrude."

"Go? We're going home, honey." He blinked a snowflake off his eyelashes and realized he'd forgotten to put on his hat.

"Okay." She didn't question, she just let him tuck her into the curve of his arm. "What about my truck? Is it safe?"

"I'll get Jud to drive it back in right now. That way you'll have your stuff. I see his truck right there. Abe can bring him back to town." He led her to his truck, pulling out his cell. He didn't want to leave her for a moment.

"Thank you." She handed him her keys, her fingers almost blue. Lord, he needed to get her gloves, boots.

"Come on, honey." He got her and Presley in the truck and sat to call Jud. He cranked the heater up, pulling his coat off and wrapping it around his baby girl.

"Oh, your truck." She grinned at him. "I even missed your truck."

"Did you? It sure is bigger than yours." Bless her heart. They'd have to get her a little bit heavier vehicle. Maybe one of them SUVs with the nice wide wheelbase.

"Yeah. It feels less…slippy."

"I bet." He took her hand when Jud answered. "Hey, buddy, do me a… Yeah. I'm still out in the lot. Abe is at the bunkhouse. Uh-huh. I'll buy you both a beer."

Rose's eyes were closed and he could see how tired she was, but there was a little smile on her lips, like she was happy and couldn't hide it.

"Thanks, man." He hung up, then waited to hand Rosie's keys over to Jud, who came up to the window. "It pulls a little to the left."

"Gotcha." Jud gave him a thumbs up, and they were off like a herd of turtles.

"Look at all that snow." She had Presley on her lap, one hand on his thigh. "And the mountains…"

"Mmm. It's pretty, huh? The house, it has a fireplace." Hopefully that would be a good thing. He'd noticed that Texans loved their fires, though God knew why. It was always hot down there.

"Yeah? I like the smell of a wood fire. Is your boss gonna be mad that I'm here?"

"No, honey. He'll be tickled." The boss wanted him to stay. A lot.

"Good. I wanted to be home with you for Thanksgiving, cook for you."

"Yeah? We gonna have something yummy?" She was dealing with everything so well. He was damned proud now that he was no longer scared to death.

"Whatever you want, plus a pecan pie." Her hand petted his leg, slow and easy. "I brought my kitchen stuff."

"You brought a whole truck. You mean it when you say you're moving in." He patted her hand before he had to shift down. "Thank God."

"I am. I mean, I can get an apartment, if you need me to, but... Les, I love you. I want to be here, with you."

"Rosie. I want you. Trust me. With me. I been fixing up the house, getting ready for you. This is a thing. No more doubts."

"Thank God." She started crying, shoulders shaking with it.

"Oh..." *Poor baby*. He wanted to hug her hard, but he had to watch the road.

"I'm okay. Just silly." She sniffled.

"You're just a little overwhelmed." The ranch road came up in no time, Les taking the turn slow and flashing his lights to let Jud know it was slippery. Rosie kept crying a little, hiccups coming from her throat.

She dried her eyes in time to see the big house. "Is that the main house? How pretty! I bet he gets lots of visitors."

"He gets a few, for sure. I keep telling him he ought to rent out rooms." Les pulled on past the big house, then the bunkhouse, heading for his little place down the way, past the hay shed.

He was a little worried that she'd be disappointed, but her face lit up when she saw the house. "Oh, Les... Is that our house?"

"It is." The lights were all on, so the place kinda glowed a little against the white everywhere. Les pulled up right next to the back door, and Jud swung around behind them.

"It's so pretty."

"It is? I mean, yeah, it is, but I'm glad you think so, too." He'd call Abe, have him come get Jud. "Come on, honey. Let you and Presley meet Iggy."

"Okay." Rosie nodded, stepped out of the truck, Presley's carrier in hand. "Can I just let him out?"

"Well, he might disappear. You can in the house, you know? I'll shovel him a path in a minute."

"I can do it, later." Rosie grinned at him. "After I have a bath, maybe."

"Honey, it will take me two minutes. He can go over here for right now, where the house hangs over." He took Presley's crate, let the little bit feel the snow before leaving him to pee.

The pup sniffed the snow, put one paw in, then started barking at it. Of course, that got Iggy to come a runnin', and next thing Les knew, Iggy had mowed Rosie down into a pile of snow, paws on her shoulders, licking her face and wagging.

"Shit!" He grabbed the heavy collar and pulled Iggy off, then picked Rosie up. Looked like Presley had piddled when the big beast had bounded out, so they could all go in and get warm and dry.

Rosie blinked up at him, her dark hair knocked loose, snowflakes dotting her eyelashes as she stared at him. "I think he likes me."

"I think he does, too. I been telling him about you."
Somehow Abe was already there to get Jud, so Jud must
have called. Les shook hands with both men briefly.
"Thanks, guys. I'll get the next round when we get
together."

"Shit. You just share some of that candy again, we'll
be even."

"I brought boxes worth, boys. There's plenty." Rosie
dusted snow off her enormous jacket.

"Hoo yeah." There was a lot of back slapping and
shit, then they were alone. "Come on, honey. I can start
a fire."

"Les, I haven't seen you in ten weeks. I don't need a
fire."

Oh.

Oh!

He grinned hugely. Right. They could warm each
other up.

He opened the door, and his girl went in, glancing
around. "Oh, Les. It's so pretty and warm and look at
the windows!"

"You like it? I didn't change the curtains any. I
figured you'd want to get them. No big roses, though."
He thought they could compromise.

"No?" she teased. "I thought you liked roses."

"They're okay. I put little ones in the guest bath, even.
We'll plant you bushes." There. Compromise.

Rosie chuckled. "The sofa is leather like the ones in
Cheyenne—I'll make some light sheer ones."

"There you go." He moved closer to her, the
weirdness of her suddenly being there falling away. He
could kiss her now.

She blinked up at him, eyes a little watery. "Home,
huh?"

"Home." Les bent, kissing her mouth, his thumbs on her cheeks to wipe her tears.

His Rosie opened up to him, sweet as sugar, tongue sliding in to touch his. Her arms slid up around his neck, and he cupped her butt, and they were cookin' with oil, all of a sudden. She was soft, in all the places a lady was supposed to be soft, and his body stiffened in response.

Les grunted, pushing Rosie all of a sudden, walking her back to the bedroom. He'd wanted to give her the whole tour, but he couldn't wait. She went easy, like she agreed with him, fingers working his flannel open. They got to the bed and Les started stripping her down. He'd had the little space heater on until he'd left, getting it nice and cozy for them to be naked.

"Pretty room." Her eyes were on him, though, that expression and those hands exploring him. "Oh, God. I've been missing you."

"I missed you, too, honey. So bad." Hell, he hadn't even realized how bad it ached, that empty spot. Not until he'd seen her again.

Her shirt came off, leaving her in a tiny black bra, a pair of jeans. *Look at her.* Les did. Look at her — that was — devouring every bit of her. God, yeah. She was it.

"Still want me?" She stepped closer, her bare belly touching his.

"Every inch." He pushed his hands up under her breasts, but that bra was in the way. Had to go. His girl was on it, though, popping the hooks free so he could feel her. Her chest was warm, not cold, but her nipples were hard as anything for him. He rubbed his thumbs over the stiff, sensitive bits of flesh, loving the little noise she made when he did. She arched for him, her head falling back a little, and it said something about how much he loved her hair that he let go of her breast with one hand to get the ponytail holder out. *There. Perfect.*

"Rosie."

She chuckled, nodded. "Please, cowboy. Love on me."

"I will. I do." He cut himself off, not willing to babble anymore. Shit. He just kissed her instead of talking. She crawled up against him, one leg hooking around him.

They rubbed, and he went for her jeans, but they were so close together that he couldn't get his hands down between their bellies.

"Bed." Such a smart girl. It would help if she moved, of course.

"Uh-huh." So he picked her up and moved her. That worked. That little bit of distance got them moved, got them getting naked.

They came back together on the bed, both of them moaning when they touched. *God. Yeah.* Her skin felt so soft, so good.

"I keep thinking I'm dreaming." She kissed him, fingers cupping his face, touching his cheeks.

"I keep thinking I'm the luckiest man on earth." He ran one hand down her back, then down over the curve of her hip.

"Oh..." She arched for him, butt pushing into his touch.

"Mmmhmm. That's it, honey. That's it." He loved the way she moved like this. So unselfconscious.

Her mouth was on his, tongue slipping inside. "Want you."

"Anything. Anything for my girl." He pushed her into a better position, spreading her good and wide.

God, she was pretty, pale skin and dark hair, all wanting and sprawled for him.

Les hummed a little, like a starving man at a feast. He kissed her mouth, then her chin, then her collarbone. "So sweet."

Her heartbeat fluttered, right under his lips, and her nipples were both dark, tight, begging for him. There was no way he could resist those. Les moved lower, taking one sweet nipple between his lips. She moaned so pretty, and her whole body went to shifting, sliding up under him. Les sucked, then licked before blowing some air against her skin. He'd learned how she liked that before, and he remembered every detail.

"Oh. Oh, I." She arched, pushed right into his mouth and he damn near died. She wanted him, so good.

Les slid a thigh between her legs, his cock rubbing along her hip. *Yeah. Oh. Damn.*

He could feel her—hot and wet and slick, her curls soft on his leg—and she was feeling him, fingers sliding over his shaft. Moaning a little more, Les rocked, nibbling at her skin. "Inside now, honey?"

"Yes." She guided him right home, rubbing that tiny bit of nerves with the tip of his cock first, which made them both gasp, shudder.

"Rosie. Oh. Missed you." Had he said that already? He figured it bore repeating when he pushed inside her. She took him, body wet and slick around him. He loved how she shuddered, how she dug her fingers into his shoulders.

They got a little crazy, both of them making these insane noises, and Les was glad he'd kicked the door shut behind them. The dogs were barking their fool heads off out there. Her fingers scratched down his back, landed on his ass to drag him in deeper and he stopped worrying about the damn dogs.

Les arched into her, his hips moving faster and faster, his balls drawing up tight. He needed her like nothing else on earth. Right now. He got one hand under her butt and tugged her up, just a little bit, and she cried out, bucked hard. *Oh, yeah. Right there.*

All he had to do now was ride it, keep hitting that perfect spot. She would go off like a bottle rocket.

"Les! Les, love!" Oh, damn. Look at her. Look at his girl. Flushed and hot, spread and pretty beneath him, body fluttering around him.

Les groaned, the sound coming from somewhere near his toes, and he bent to kiss her, his mouth needing to be on hers. He felt every second of her orgasm, and she cried out, right into their kiss.

His body jerked, his cock pushing deep as he came inside her. He couldn't even hold on long enough to watch her pretty face.

"Les." She held him close, breath huffing from her.

"Uh-huh. This is the bedroom."

"I like it." She smiled at him, corners of her eyes crinkling.

"You like the bed? I know you like it a little softer, so I got one of them pillow-top things."

Rosie teared up, hand on his cheek. "So good to me, cowboy."

"What? I wanted to blackmail you into coming up." He grinned, feeling like he was ten feet tall.

"I couldn't wait anymore. I needed to be home with you."

"I'm glad, honey. So glad." Les kissed Rosie's mouth, loving the taste of her, the feel of her in their bed. "Welcome home."

If she cried a little before she curled up in his arms and slept, that didn't matter one bit.

Not one bit.

Chapter Twenty-Eight

Rosie sat at the kitchen table, a steaming cup of tea in her hands. Apparently Hester Anne, who was Les' sister, had told him to make sure he had hot tea when she arrived. She would need it.

Thank goodness, because the steam soothed her nose and the honey in the tea coated her dry throat. The air here could freeze nose hair in seconds, it was so frigid and arid at the same time.

Les had left her in bed and gone to unload as much of her truck as he could, and Rosie had gotten up to help. Les had carried her back inside, plopped her down, then made her tea. He didn't seem mad. Maybe... Well, he'd been scared for her, she thought.

When he came in with her big suitcase, he shook off snow and finally took off his hat again. "I tarped up the rest of your boxes, hon and moved your truck under the carport. That ought to keep us until the storm is over."

"Thank you, love." She smiled, her chin only quivering a little. "Are you— Did I make you mad?"

"No, honey." He smiled and it reached his eyes so she knew he was telling the truth. Then he squatted in front of her, taking her hands in his cold ones. "Now, I got something to say, and you need to let me get it out."

Worry lodged in her belly. "Oh. Okay. What?"

"I love you, sweet lady. I have never been so happy to see anyone. But if you ever pull another harebrained stunt like this one again in my lifetime, I will beat you or something equally crazy, do you understand? You took ten years off my life in the last two weeks."

"What?" She almost kicked him when she stood abruptly, staring down at him. "What do you mean?"

"Beau called me and told me you were leaving, honey. I was real patient because he said you wanted to surprise me. I didn't even lose it when you broke down in Omaha. But the flat as the last straw."

She stared at him, mouth falling open in shock. "You knew? All this time?" Oh, she was going to kick Beau's ass.

"I did. I'm so proud, and as long as you kept up the ruse I was gonna keep on, but don't you ever do that to me again. You hear? Never doubt that I want you."

Rose burst into tears, unable to stop herself. She wept, great, heaving sobs that relieved all the fear and stress of the last ten days. When the storm ended, she slapped his chest, furious that she'd done all this secret stuff for nothing. "I can't believe you knew and you didn't tell me!"

"Well, that's what we get for trying to keep secrets from each other, right?" He stroked her hair, then kissed her forehead. "No more of that, right?"

Rose twined her fingers with his, which had warmed right up. "I promise, cowboy. Never again."

"Good deal. How about breakfast for supper?"

"Bacon makes everything better," she agreed.

"You sit, honey. I'll cook this time. Tomorrow you can make me sweets."

Rose chuckled, feeling wrung out enough to agree. "You got yourself a deal, cowboy. Bring on breakfast."

* * * *

Les watched Rosie sleep, so glad she was safe.

He'd fed her, then tucked her in early, and Presley and Iggy had watched over her while she slept until he got the chores done. Good dogs.

Now he had stripped down and climbed into bed with her, her pale skin hidden by layers of sweatpants and sweaters. She'd get used to the cold, and he could turn up the heat.

Tomorrow. Oh, tomorrow he would have a surprise for her that he hoped rivaled the one she'd wanted to give him. He'd waited so long for the right time. Now seemed good.

Poor baby. She was so tired she hadn't even had a look at the house. He hoped she liked it, for sure. There was still a lot to do, but those things were all little female touches that she would want to put on the place herself. God knew she was good at that.

"Oh, Rosie girl, I swear you'll never regret it."

Les bent down to kiss her forehead, and she smiled in her sleep as if she knew he was there with her. Yeah. Tomorrow was the day. He was gonna ask her to marry him.

Chapter Twenty-Nine

Rosie laughed at Iggy as he bounded through the snow after Presley, the huge beast fascinated by her baby. The morning had dawned clear and cold and wonderful, and a bunch of hands had come by to unload her truck, the boss's wife sending down cinnamon buns and bacon enough for a working.

She had a cup of coffee, two pairs of Les' socks on, and her kitchen unpacked. There was a Texas sheet cake in the oven, a pot roast on the stove, and all she had left to do was unpack her bathroom stuff.

In their pretty house. The house Les had made up for her.

Three bedrooms, a bathroom and a half, a wee baby back porch. The kitchen wasn't big, but she loved it a little. Maybe more than a little.

God, look at all that white out there.

Les came in the back door, stomping snow off his boots. He stopped short when he saw her, his face splitting in a huge smile. "Hey, honey."

"Hey, baby. How did the feeding go? Do you want coffee?" God, he was fine as frog hair.

"Cold. But everyone can get through, now." He toed his boots off. He'd promised her they'd go when the roads cleared and get her a good winter pair.

"There's pot roast. It'll be ready in half an hour." She poured him a cup, handed it over before snatching Presley up in an old towel to dry him off. Snow was *wet*. And Presley was so furry.

"Smells good, honey. So does the sweet. It's not candy, though, huh?" The boys had eaten most of the caramels when they'd dropped by to meet her. Les was looking like a hungry cat.

"Not today. I have to go grocery shopping. It's chocolate cake though."

"I like cake." He put his cold hands right on her, right above her jeans on her waist.

"Les!" She squeaked and jumped, landing right in his arms.

"Mmm. See, I have an ulterior motive." He laughed, rubbing his stubbly cheek against her neck.

She stretched and wiggled, chuckling with him. "I unpacked most everything, got a couple of pictures hung and all. It's so pretty here."

"You like it? I can't wait to take you out. Maybe go riding."

"I'd love that." She kissed him, slow and easy, just about perfectly happy.

"We got to go into town, get you outfitted first." They had to go get groceries and all, too, and he'd promised her a little Christmas shopping. She wanted to get something Colorado for Beau and Sam.

"Sounds perfect." She kissed the tip of his nose. "There's a few minutes left on the roast, baby. Come talk to me while I do the last bit of unpacking?"

She didn't want to miss any time with him, not right now.

"Sure." He took her hand and let her lead him to the bathroom, settling on the pot with the lid down while she started pulling things out of her train case. "I didn't do much in here. Figured you'd want to."

"I like the color a lot, but I think I'll get a prettier shower curtain." The room was a sweet pale yellow, but the shower curtain was just a white plastic thing. She was thinking just to add a little sheer on top would be nicer.

She pulled out her makeup kit and got it organized on the counter. Her toothbrush was beside Les', her hairbrush was in the bathroom drawer and she put her hairdryer under the sink.

"I thought about getting the one with the daisies, but I was worried it would be cheesy." Les' legs looked so funny in the tiny room, like they had nowhere to go.

"I like daisies. Maybe we should just have something simple, a little see-through." She cut her eyes over, glanced at him. "You're awful fine, all wet in the shower."

She put her Midol, her birth control pills, and her mousse in the medicine cabinet.

His cheeks heated, and his eyes twinkled at her. "So are you. I like you a little soapy." Les stood, reaching over her oh-so-casually and grabbing her birth control. Which he then threw in the trash. "We'll have to get a trash can with a lid, too."

She arched her eyebrow, her heart going a little faster. "Okay. We'll pick one up."

She moved closer to him, right into his arms.

"Those we're not gonna need anymore." He grinned, holding her close.

"No? You sure, cowboy?" She could handle that. Les' babies. She remembered Lindsay saying.

"I'm real sure, honey. You through putting stuff up? I got something to show you."

"I am." She shut the medicine cabinet, grabbed the empty box. "Lead the way, Mister Les."

He grabbed her hand again, and this time he led, back to the front room. He called it the living room. He got into a box next to the fireplace, and he didn't get down on one knee or anything, but she knew what was coming right off. Rose couldn't help but smile, though, knowing her cowboy so good. Being his was what she wanted, more than anything.

"I been wanting to ask, but I wanted to wait until we were face to face. I do love you, honey. Marry me?" His eyes crinkled up, and he smiled so sweet.

"Yes, sir. I'd love to."

"Oh, good." Les opened the little ring box, and it was a simple gold band with a single diamond. Nothing big and showy, and nothing that would get caught when she worked in the kitchen.

Les was her practical cowboy, so different than Timmy.

She'd had Timmy's ring turned into a little pendant, a rose with diamond leaves. Les had helped her pick the design. Rose held out her hand. "Put it on me?"

"Yes, ma'am." He fumbled some, but he got it on her, sliding it on her left ring finger. It sparkled when she turned her hand. "Look at that."

"Looks like it belongs." Felt good, too. She liked being someone's wife.

"It does. Awful pretty." He brought her hand to his mouth and kissed the backs of her fingers.

"I love you, Les." Her fingers curled around his.

"Good. It would suck if you didn't." Les kissed her on the mouth then, slow and soft.

She stepped close, his fingers easing the clip out of her hair, letting it fall down loose. Les moaned, combing his fingers through the heavy mass. He did love her hair, bless his heart.

The kiss stole her breath plumb away, made her heart beat hard in her chest.

They broke apart when the beeper on the oven went off. Les smiled. "Roast needs to rest."

"You remembered." He'd teased her something awful the first time she'd told him that.

"I do. Why don't you go take it out and I'll go wash up." He winked. "I might need you to come help me change my shirt or something. In a minute."

He handed her the little ring box and headed for the bedroom. There was a little piece of paper hanging out the back, a piece of the receipt.

She didn't care about how much he paid, but she couldn't help but notice that the address was a jeweler in Dallas. He'd bought the ring before he'd ever left Texas.

Rose smiled, settled in her soul. Home. She was home.

Epilogue

The wedding went real well, at least as far as Les was concerned. He didn't pass out when Rosie came down the aisle. He didn't make a fool of himself with the first dance at the reception. And he didn't fall over dead when Ace Porter, the king of the cowboys himself, came to give him their wedding present. Les figured it was bad manners to scream the amount of the check out loud, but that was sure what he wanted to do. He knew his eyes had bugged out like a cartoon, for sure.

Jesus, it was like he'd married into royalty or something.

Rosie was out on the dance floor in her jeans and her white shirt, her hair down and loose, tiny white flowers sprinkled in the dark mass. Beau Lafitte had danced with her, then Krese Peirson and Coke Pharris. Now the four-time entertainer of the year Dillon Walsh was dancing her around, making her laugh.

Look at her.

Everything else went away for a moment, and all he could see was his Rosie. She was so pretty. So his. All official like. He might just break down and blubber he was so proud and happy.

She glanced over at him, those dark eyes landing on him like a touch, and she waved, smiled.

"She sure loves you, Lester."

Hester Anne settled beside him, looking pretty as a picture in her pink Western shirt and silver buckle with roses on it. All of them in the wedding party had one. Timmy's mom and dad had insisted. They were amazing folks, and had come to give his girl away since her own momma and daddy had passed on.

"Well, that's a good thing, huh?" Les grinned at his sister, nudging her with his elbow. "'Cause she married me, and I'm working on getting her knocked up."

"Man, you are a fucking delicate flower. Mamma'd love you to have babies, sure enough." She whacked him, hard. "Your boss thinks she's a miracle worker. A winter wonderland for the bull riding crowd, he says. Renting out cabins, he says..."

"Christ." Les glanced around. "Did you see who all is here?" He was rodeo enough to want to dance a jig at the names on the guest list.

"Yeah." His sister grinned at him. "What's cool is that she doesn't. She's only looking at you."

"I know." Les' eye went right back to Rosie, who was sort of dangling from Dillon Walsh's arm in a dip all of a sudden. "She's got the most loyal friends. Makes me proud to know so many people think she's a good'un, you know?"

Hester nodded, and they watched the dancing a while longer. Rosie's laugh came more and more often, and she'd been making enough with her candy business to start a 'having our baby' fund. Practical, pretty, and all his. Then Hester Anne popped his arm again. "Go dance with her, brother."

"Huh? Oh. Sure." Les laughed when Hes crossed her eyes at him and stuck out her tongue, just like when they were kids. Then he hoisted himself up and went over, tapping Dillon Walsh's shoulder. "I'm cutting in, sir."

Dillon hemmed and hawed playfully, but the man deposited his wife right into his arms. Rosie smiled up at him. "Having a good day, Mister Les?"

"I am. Possibly the best ever. How are you holding up?" She looked amazing. Happy. So his. Did he mention she was his? Love filled him all up, his heart beating hard.

"I'm having a ball. Ready for our honeymoon, though." She kissed him. "You, me, Mexico."

They were going to one of them all-inclusive resort deals, swim-up bar and all. Rosie in a bikini and lotion and nothing else.

"Yeah? We could leave it all to Ace and the boss..." He was ready to slip out of the crowd.

"Our suitcases are in your truck, so's my purse with the passports and tickets." Jesus bless them both, she looked so pretty, smiling up at him.

"Well, come on." They'd say goodbye to Hes and the family, and to Beau and Sam, because Beau had been good enough to sponsor her side of the wedding. Oh, and the boss, because he'd let them use the big lodge.

"Right beside you, love."

Lord, Les did love a woman who knew her own mind, and was willing to just go for it. 'Course that had been what he'd loved about Rosie from the very beginning.

She'd known she was the one for him. Thank God for that.

About the Author

Texan to the bone and an unrepentant Daddy's Girl, BA spends her days with her basset hounds, getting tattooed, texting her sisters, and eating Mexican food. When she's not doing that, she's writing. She spends her days off watching rodeo, knitting and surfing Pinterest in the name of research. BA's personal saviors include her wife, Julia, her best friend, Sean, and coffee. Lots of good coffee.

BA loves to hear from readers. You can find her contact information, website and author biography at http://www.totallybound.com.

TOTALLY
BOUND

Home of Erotic Romance